THE DREAMER OF DREAMS
BY THE QUEEN OF ROUMANIA
ILLUSTRATED BY EDMUND DULAC

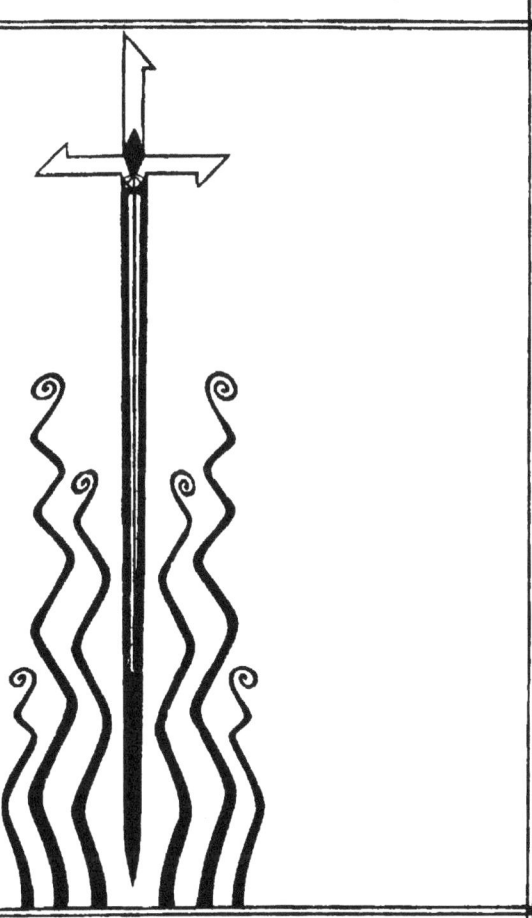

HODDER & STOUGHTON • LONDON • NEW YORK • TORONTO

Dedicated

TO MY DAUGHTER

ILEANA

"I LOOKED INTO HER EYES AND THEREIN
I SAW HOPES AND DREAMS AND ALL THE
PROMISES LIFE CONTAINS."

ILLUSTRATIONS

	PAGE
EVERYTHING ABOUT HER WAS WHITE, GLISTENING AND SHINING	17
ERIC LAY NOW, STRETCHED AT THE FEET OF THE WOMAN HE COULD NOT LEAVE	39
A CIRCLE OF MIST SEEMED TO BE SETTLING AROUND THEM	72
IT WAS THE MIRACULOUS BUBBLES	100
AND THERE, LEANING AGAINST A MOSS-GROWN CRUMBLING TREE, WAS A SPIRIT-LIKE BEING OUT OF ANOTHER WORLD!	125
KING WANDA SAT UPON HIS MARBLE TERRACE BASKING IN THE FIRST WARMTH OF THE SEASON	173

I

And I dream in my waking dreams, and deep in the dreams of sleep.
                                            FIONA MACLEOD

CONSTERNATION reigned in King Wanda's castle,—the great Northern King before whose will so many trembled, before whose smile so many crouched in expectation. His favourite painter had suddenly lost his wits and refused to finish the picture he had begun on the walls of the ancient hall where all the great banquets were held—a beautiful hall, where a frieze was being conjured into life by the incomparable art of Eric Gundian, a quite young man of wonderful talent, who had been discovered by the King one sunshiny morning.

Each day that Eric Gundian had spent within the King's walls his reputation had grown, and he had, all unconsciously, become the Court favourite. His every whim had been an order; and his gay handsome face had been loved by old and young.

The creeping jealousies around him had died down of themselves before the sweetness of his smile and the wonder of his art.

The sound of his voice was like spring birds singing of love in green-clad forests, and when the sun shone on his head it was like the haze of a summer's evening over a ripe cornfield. In his eyes slumbered the beautiful peace of mountain lakes, and in his heart there lived the simple trust of a pure soul . . . and now Eric Gundian, Eric of the golden locks—Eric the fairy-fingered, Eric the sweet-voiced had lost his wits!

One morning he awoke, and no one could understand the meaning of his talk; he declared he had had a dream, and in his dream he had seen two eyes, the eyes he needed for the completing of his picture; and without those eyes he never again could touch either colour or brush. King Wanda had called for him to be brought before his presence, but Eric had sullenly refused to answer his command.

At first King Wanda had been furiously angry, but then he remembered Eric's wonderful art, and had deigned to go out to where his favourite sat on the cool marble steps, that led down to the lake, before the King's white palace of beauty.

Eric had risen before the crowned figure that bent towards him a stern face of inquiry, but to all the King's questions, to all his persuasions, flatteries, threats, and entreaties Eric had replied with a sad gesture of resignation, that never again could he take up his brush till he had found those eyes which had haunted his dream. His pain and his despair were so evident, that King Wanda felt that no words had force to move the distracted young man. Sadly he departed, and mounted one by one the shallow marble steps which reflected in glowing colours the costly clothes that he wore. Once more he turned and looked down upon his favourite, who sat, his head in his hands, gazing across the sparkling lake; he heaved a deep sigh and felt like quarrelling with Fate who had despoiled him of one of his great joys.

As he reached the palace door, he was met by the sweet little figure of his daughter, who came out into the sunshine, gathering up her long trailing dress, a golden ball clasped in her hands. The King smiled upon her, and bade her go down to the water's edge to try and console the young painter with her radiant youth. With a gay laugh Oona rolled her golden ball down the snow-white steps, and it fell with a splash into the water at the young man's feet, making great circles that spread, always widening, over the blue expanse ; but Eric never moved, he kept staring into the distance as if he were following a vision no other eye could see. Oona came noiselessly down the steps, rather awed by the silence and stillness of the young man who had always been her gayest playfellow.

Gently she drew near to where he sat, and dropped down at his side—then like a playful kitten she nestled quite close to him and peered up into his face. The smile faded from her soft lips and gave way to a look of wonder and distress. She put both arms round her young friend's neck, and pressing her blossom-like cheek against his shoulder, she asked him gently if he would not come and play with her beneath the flowering apple-trees.

Eric looked at her as if she were a stranger ; his eyes seemed to wander over her fair face without any recognition. Suddenly little Oona was afraid, and drew back ; what had come to her friend ? Why was he so changed ? Why did she begin to shiver in the warm sunshine so that all around her lost light and colour ?

Once more she drew near, her warm little heart longing to help, longing to bring the smile back to the eyes of her companion. She wore a dark-red rose in her belt, and drawing it out she pulled the red petals off, one by one, letting them drop over his bent head down upon the white marble at his feet. But Eric never looked up ; the velvety petals lay, a fading little heap, unnoticed upon the marble step, till a small gust of wind swept them into the water which carried them away far out of sight.

Poor little Oona rose to her feet; a great fear had come over her; and gathering up her long white skirts she fled back into the palace as if she were being pursued.

Still Eric sat, gazing into space, till night came down and blotted out all things from his sight.

II

I run across hills and dales, I wander through nameless lands . . . because I am hunting for a golden dream.

TAGORE.

THE road was long and dusty, and stretched out before the wanderer's feet. He carried a small wallet on his back, and in his hand was a strong stick. The little birds on the trees sang glad songs because it was spring-time, and the branches were weighed down by the wealth of their blossoms. The wanderer was young, and his face was good to look upon; his clothes were new, and round his neck he wore a golden chain which was the royal gift of a King. His step was light and eager, and there was a look of hope in his eyes; he had a flute in his pocket upon which he played from time to time a sweet little tune—a little tune the end notes of which always sounded like an unanswered question.

None had been able to keep him back; Eric of the golden locks, . . . Eric the fairy-fingered, . . . Eric the sweet-voiced, . . . Eric the mad painter, had left the white castle of beauty, to wander the wide world over seeking for two eyes that had come to him in a dream.

In the great hall King Wanda stood, looking on the unfinished frieze; it was a marvellous painting in glowing colours that ran all round the room. A master hand alone could have been capable of such perfect composition, such rich colouring, such charm and poetry. The great procession represented the triumph of Love.

It was like a wondrous wedding-feast, and all the figures were moving, an army of joyous youths and maidens, towards a golden throne. On the throne sat a woman whose golden robe flowed, like a river seen at sunset, down towards the youths and maidens who were singing songs of praise, whilst they swung bloom-laden branches over their heads and cast white roses before the throne of Love. Behind this vision of youth came stern-faced warriors on snorting chargers, and pearl-crowned queens who led golden-haired children by the hand. Then came musicians who were followed by troops of beggars and the tattered forms of the poor, all hurrying, pressing, streaming towards that golden throne. . . . But the woman on the throne had no face.

The fairy fingers of the artist had stopped here, suddenly; before the final accomplishment, which was to have crowned his whole masterpiece, Eric's brush had failed him. In his dreams he had seen the face he wanted, the eyes that haunted him; but the moment he woke his vision paled, and no effort of will could call back the look of those eyes which he needed for the woman on the throne.

So Eric—the Eric whom every one loved, who had been the stern King's joy—had gone mad because of the desire for those eyes of his dream.

The light began to fail in the great hall; still King Wanda stood gazing at the figure on the throne which had no face. Great rage seized him because of his helplessness, and a great longing for the fair-haired youth who had been his joy and pride. Little Oona came up to where he stood, and slipped her cool hand into his, laying her curly head against his arm. He turned to her with a deep sigh, and together they passed out into the flowering garden.

The wanderer sped along the endless road always farther and farther from the palace of the King. His shoes were covered with dust, and when his steps began to lag he would take from his pocket the flute upon which he played that sad little tune with the questioning notes at the end.

It was mid-day—Eric had already walked many miles, and now the sun beat down with great force on his head. He wondered where he was, but only vaguely, because since his dream he seemed to have another head on his shoulders, and none of the tidy thoughts of other days would come to him. He had no notion where he was going ; he only knew that he could not rest until he found that face he needed for his picture, and above all those great eyes that haunted his dreams.

He sat very still at the edge of the road where he had thrown himself. He closed his eyes, and the moment he did so those he was seeking were before him, great and luminous, with an expression he had never seen in any other look. How clear they were, and how steadfastly they rested upon him with never a droop of the eyelids. It did not strike him that he might be on a fool's errand, he had no doubts and no fears ; the great genius had become like to a little child, confident and with no thoughts of failure. He had no plan, he simply meant to travel all the world over till he found what he was seeking ; God would care for him as He did for the birds of the air, and time did not count. He wiped his damp brow, and then looked about him ; all was very still, the air was laden with the sweet perfumes of summer flowers ; the sky was blue, and not a leaf stirred on the trees. Eric smiled to himself, and played on his flute ; he liked to listen to his own little tunes ; they were very sweet to him, and he quite forgot everything whilst he piped away like a bird. He began many different melodies, but they always ended on the same questioning notes. He never remarked that each of his little tunes had the same ending ; to him they were infinitely varied. And intensely sweet they were, with a haunting sound like human sighs mixed with the laughter of little children. And now the clearest bird notes rang out, and then again the sob of a nightingale or the trickling sound of running water, clear and crystalline, as if a little source were bubbling forth close by. He was completely absorbed by the music, and more than one passer-by had stopped a moment to listen ; but Eric had only nodded and smiled as if each one had been a personal acquaintance.

Then he rose and wandered onwards, always keeping straight along the road that stretched before him, never inquiring his way, serenely confident that all would go well with him if he only held his one great aim in view.

Before the King's palace Oona, flitting hither and thither, like a gay butterfly, played with her golden balls in the sunshine, occasionally tripping over her too royal apparel, her clear laugh sounding through the summer-laden air.

But within the still, white palace sat King Wanda, and all the time his eyes beheld a small cloud of dust, raised by the feet of a golden-haired youth, who had been the joy of his days, leaving him and all his kingly splendour to follow a vision which the grey-haired man could never understand,—and it seemed to him that the little cloud of dust became always smaller and smaller till he could see it no more.

III

From my heart comes out and dances before me the image of my desire.
                                                                        TAGORE.

THE town was tiny and the streets so narrow that conversation could be held by neighbours across the road beneath the gables. The high pointed roofs had all the shades of red and brick, and before nearly each small window bunches of scarlet geraniums bloomed in profusion,—a sleepy little place, where the grey cats lazily slept in the middle of the pavement quite undisturbed by any passer-by, quite safe from being run over. They blinked their eyes in the bright sunshine, and stretched their supple limbs to the kindly warmth.

Over the sea of red roofs the different-shaped chimneys sent up their bluish smoke that hung like a transparent cloud waving slowly backwards and forwards in the still air. Now steps came along one of the quiet streets, and the silence was such that they were heard long before the walker came into sight. He was a quite young man, tired but light of step, and his uncovered head shone like gold in the sunshine. Round his neck he wore a heavy golden chain, and his clothes were new; within his eyes there was a searching look, but a smile was on his face, and the world seemed to him just one long road upon which he could follow his dream. He chose the shady side of the street because the day was warm and the sun had poured down for many hours upon his way.

All the time he glanced right and left as if expecting to find what he was looking for; but he was in no hurry, and often a glad little song broke from his lips, whilst the sound of his strong stick on the cobble stones had a cheery note that echoed along the houses. Eric felt like a bird of the air, that could fly whither it would, and for which each tree was a resting-place.

He cared little for how long he had wandered, nor for what he had left behind, nor where he was going ; all he needed was a long road that would lead him on and on until he reached his goal. And his goal might be reached any day, any hour, any minute. Hope was always within his heart ; but it mattered not if its fulfilment were to-day or to-morrow.

His smile was so sweet and his face so fair that all were ready to open their doors to him ; so he feared neither hunger nor thirst, neither heat nor cold, neither night nor storm.

Now he was feeling rather weary, so he sat down on a door-step, drew his flute from his pocket, and began to play soft little runs up and down ; his fingers, as if they were dancing, moving lightly over the small holes.

The flies buzzed around him trying to tease him, but he was indifferent to all except the sweet notes of his flute. So absorbed was he that he did not hear the door open behind him, and only looked up when a hand was laid upon his shoulder.

'Twas the trembling hand of a quite old woman, very bent, her face lined with many wrinkles, her eyes dim and tired. Eric sprang to his feet and craved pardon for being in her way.

She looked hard at him, at first with annoyance ; but his wonderful smile disarmed her, so she hobbled away shaking her head, turning round more than once to look again at the youthful stranger. She had left the door into the crooked little house wide open.

Eric sat down once more upon the steps and continued his music. It was wonderful the peace it gave him ; he needed nothing else—did not even try to think, leaving Fate to shape events around him.

From the upper window trails of scarlet geraniums hung down over his head ; a faint breeze fanned them, making some loose petals fall upon his knees.

With a smile he gathered them in his hand, enjoying the beauty of their colour, letting them drop through his fingers, playing with them like a child.

And now from inside the house he caught sounds of a sweet voice singing softly some old, old song. The notes rose and rose until they entirely filled the small house behind him.

He looked up to the window, but could see only the red flowers against the rusty old wall.

He rose and stood in the doorway, and listened to the voice that sounded like a bird singing in a wood, singing, singing to its mate a song of Love.

It did not make his heart beat as it would have done the hearts of other youths, but it dawned upon him that the voice was human, and that it could only belong to a girl or a woman.

Thoughts came but slowly to him as through a mist, because we know that since that fatal morning Eric Gundian had lost his wits.

But Eric Gundian was still, to all outward appearance, the same beautiful young man, with the same face, the same golden hair, the same luminous smile that bespoke the simple trust of a pure soul. . . . Now, moved by some irresistible impulse, Eric walked into the house, and, led by the glorious voice, climbed the narrow dark stairs, up, up, as if he were mounting into the skies. Then before the open door of a small sunlit room, he suddenly paused, seized with wonder. . . .

Sitting near the window, her fair head bent over her work, was a lovely maiden : she drew stitch after stitch through the snow-white linen, and the hand which held the shining thread moved backwards and forwards like a dove hovering over a gateway.

As she worked the song burst from her lips; she sang and sang, with the glorious gladness of youth which has not yet known either sorrow or disappointment. There was nothing sad in her tune, it was all hope and joy and sweetness. Behind her head the geraniums made a fiery haze where the sun smote upon them with the blinding rays of summer. Then it was that Gundian felt all his soul awake with the longing that she would look up, so that he might see her eyes. . . .

Perhaps they would be the eyes he was searching for. To-day, to-morrow, this hour, or the next he was sure to meet them.

The maiden, all unconscious of his presence, sang on and on, from one song to another, the sweetness of her voice ringing through the stillness like glad Easter bells.

The wanderer held his breath; and, both hands pressed against his breast, waited in a sort of agony for her to raise her head.

At last she did so, but it was towards the window she looked.

She even left her chair and reached far out over the red geraniums to glance into the street below.

As she sat down her eyes turned to the door where the stranger stood watching. With a little cry of fear she crumpled the white linen against her and stared at him without finding a word.

Impulsively Eric sprang forward, and taking her with a quick movement by both shoulders, he whirled her round to the light, peering with a hungry longing into her eyes. . . . All was done in a flash; the astonished girl was so taken by surprise that she had no time to defend herself against so sudden an onslaught.

But hardly had he seen her eyes than he let her go again, and putting his two hands over his face, with a cry of disappointment, he turned and fled.

Down the dark narrow stairs he sped, out into the bright sunlight ; there he paused a moment to pick up his stick and flute, then ran as if possessed ; and before long he had left the sleepy red-roofed little town far behind. . . . Still he ran, ran, eager to get away from the eyes which were not the eyes he wanted.

IV

I have come far, led by my dreams and visions.
TAGORE

THE moon was shining down upon an endless expanse of snow —as far as the eye could reach, snow, snow, white and dazzling, strewn with a million glittering diamonds.

It had ceased snowing; the storm was over; but the wind still blew in biting blasts, forcing the wanderer to draw his cloak more closely around him, and to bend his head, as he slowly advanced over that everlasting desert of white.

He walked and walked; there was no end to this frozen snow-field over which his feet had made a narrow little path that alone disturbed the shroud-like surface. And always longer and longer it grew, zigzagging beneath the quiet face of the moon.

From time to time the wind blew snowflakes against him, and they beat in his face like a thousand pins, obliging him to shut his eyes not to be blinded.

Each flake had another shape; there were stars and crosses, moss-like flowers and strangely shaped butterflies, all dancing in mad circles around the lonely wayfarer.

Some kept their beautiful shape even when fallen to the ground, and the moon would light them up like precious jewels out of a queenly casket.

The young man was the only living thing in this wilderness of ice and snow.

He could not have told how he had got there; what will was

driving him always onwards upon his mad search ; but nothing had power to stop him, nor had fear any place in his soul.

Now, even the wind died down and a hush fell over all things.

The light of the moon became intenser in the growing stillness.

Looking up, Eric saw myriads of stars twinkling down upon him from unknown heights, like friendly eyes encouraging him on his way. For a moment he stood still ; the silence was now as overpowering as the storm had been ; everything around him was bathed in a cold hard light, the whiteness of which ceaselessly burnt into his brain. Suddenly a little bluey flame came dancing out of the distance, then another, and another, always more numerous, till the whole expanse was covered with them ; a wavering army of little lights, like thousands of lost souls coming together for a last parade in this land of the forgotten. Eric tried to seize one with his frozen fingers, but no sooner had he thought to grasp it than it slid away like a shape in a dream.

Then with childlike eagerness he began a mad chase after the elusive little flames, running to and fro in the moonlight in an effort to catch them, yet never succeeding ; there were always more and more lights tempting him onwards over that desert of snow.

At last he laughed aloud, standing still to watch the little blue flames float away into the unknown out of which they had come, one after another like a long procession of pilgrims in the night. . . .

They became always smaller and smaller, seeming to beckon to him as they disappeared, inviting him to follow once more in a mad chase over the hard frozen snow.

A glow had spread over Eric's cheeks, his eyes sparkled, and the moon reflected herself within them. He uncovered his head, throwing back his golden locks with a boyish gesture, whilst he stood still to watch the wonder of this northern night so clear and dazzling.

As he waited with arms outstretched trying to grasp all the beauty to his heart, the artist in him keenly alive to his surroundings, he discerned a shadow approaching, followed by a second and then a third. And as they came nearer he realized that they were great white bears hardly to be distinguished from their background.

Our wanderer felt no thrill of fear, the great beasts were so completely in keeping with their surroundings; their white skins harmonized perfectly with the immaculate snow. They came slowly towards him, quiet and majestic, slightly swinging their heavy bodies as they glided onwards. He could count about twenty.

Their huge soft feet marked also a little road on the even surface which would soon join the one Eric had made from the opposite direction. Now they were quite near; their warm breath made little clouds before them that surrounded their pointed heads like a mist.

Eric watched, fascinated, and made no movement to get out of their way.

The first reached him, and without taking the slightest notice passed on, making a small circle, but did not pause in his quiet march; and the others followed in the traces his feet had left behind him, ten, twenty, thirty. Eric counted them and always more and more came noiselessly over the snow.

But now there was another shape rising out of the distance, apparently as white as the watchful animals that led the way, the form of a tall woman whose garments fell around her in glittering folds.

Eric could not yet discern her features, she was too far off;

but he saw how more than once she paused, bending down to gather from the snow something which she held within her hands, gazing upon it with curious intensity.

Nearer and nearer she glided, her bare feet hardly touching the ground. She seemed shaped out of floating mists.

All the splendour of the night, the dazzling brilliancy, the vast snow-field, the glory of the moon, the myriad stars, all paled before the beauty of the woman that now approached.

Everything about her was white, glistening and shining; so shining that the human eye could hardly bear the radiance. Her long white hair hung about her; a circle of glow-worms surrounded her forehead. Her head was bent, still gazing on that which she held in her hand. On either side marched one of the great bears like two guardians. Just as she neared the spot where Eric stood she once more bent to the snow, and with almost loving precaution raised something in her hand.

As she did so her eyes met Eric's—they were beautiful eyes—large, dark, blazing like two burning coals. The young man felt a great emotion when they rested upon him, yet he knew directly that they were not the eyes he was seeking; but greatly did he long to know who the beautiful woman was, and what she was gathering in the snow.

As if guessing his thoughts she spoke in a clear, soft voice, always keeping her eyes fixed on his, " Thou wouldst know who I am, O lonely wanderer? I am the queen of these vast regions of snow—my home is yonder, where none dare dwell—and on nights when the moon shines bright I come out of my castle of ice and wander over this desert of white, searching for the broken hearts that have been banished here. It is only when the moon shines bright that I can find them, for they are hidden so far and wide that in the dark nights I could not see them,—and in the day never can I wander about,

—the night alone is made for me. See, I will show thee those I have found."

And opening her hand, Eric perceived three little pulsing hearts, beating, beating like frightened birds—and each little heart was broken, and drops of blood stained the white fingers of the snow-maiden.

She leant towards them and very gently touched them with her lips.

"I carry them home with me," continued the strange woman, "and I put them there where they are safe, and where they can await God's last call. I send my little dancing lights before me, and my ice bears walk with me everywhere. They come from great distances; the moment the moon shines bright they all assemble before my palace to let me know it is time for me to begin my search. They make my way, so that I should not go where the snow is too deep, or where the ice would wound my feet.

"Come! if thou art not afraid, and I shall show thee where I keep my precious treasure of broken hearts."

Stretching her hand out to the young man, she clasped his, and he found himself being drawn along across the great white plain, quicker, always quicker—till all was but a mist before his eyes; yet he felt that even if it were to death he was being hurried he could not but follow this wonderful vision of the night.

Faster and faster became their pace.

Eric hardly knew how he was moving; on both sides of them ran the white bears keeping step with their racing.

All of a sudden his beautiful guide stopped.

And pointing before her Eric looked . . . and there, rising out of the mist, hanging in the air, was a gigantic castle, built out of ice, that glittered and sparkled above the clouds—a marvellous sight, the dream-like vision of another world.

The snow-maiden again seized her companion's hand, and now she was leading him up a thousand slippery steps, hewn out of ice, that seemed to wind through the clouds. Eric's breath came in gasps; but still on rushed the fair woman, as with winged feet, till they reached a large space before the palace portals.

They stood wide open, and from within streamed forth a blue light that gleamed far out over the smooth snow. "Come," said the snow-maiden, and she put her finger to her lips.

Still holding Eric by the hand, she led him through the wide-open doors into a vast hall, made of ice and snow. Great columns supported the domed roof, and the windows that were of transparent ice gave a strange blue light that filled the whole place.

The hall was quite empty; the floor was put together out of small pieces of ice forming wonderful patterns that shimmered in different shades of white. In the middle a small descending staircase interrupted the smooth surface— a sort of dark well, the first steps of which shone bluish and ghost-like. A great light came up from somewhere far down in the heart of the earth.

The snow-maiden, still tightly clasping Eric's hand, now began to descend the narrow stairs, and the deeper they went the stronger became the light, till they reached a low vaulted chamber of great size and quite round, in the middle of which burnt a blinding circle of light. At first Eric was too bewildered to grasp the meaning of that ring of flame; then he recognized the little tongues of fire that had mocked him out yonder in the wilderness. The snow-maiden had sunk on her knees, and beckoning Eric to come nearer, she raised one of the little fluttering blazes that remained balanced on her hand like a luminous butterfly.

Eric stared, his head close to his beautiful companion's,

and saw a small hole made in the snow, where lay a tiny red heart which was split right across.

"This," whispered the snow-maiden, "is the heart of a poor little child, whose mother abandoned it, and who died of grief. I found it several years ago.

"Every day I come here to all my hearts, so that they shall not feel lonely; and these little flames are their guardians. Each little will-o'-the-wisp protects one of the hearts and keeps it warm, so that it shall not perish.

"And see! This one is my favourite, but it is very difficult to keep alive because it spent its life too rapidly, too passionately. It is the heart of a poet and a lover; a lover whose passion was so violent that he died quite suddenly, one flower-scented night, when his hope had been torn from him, and his heart broke right in two. Behold I had to bind it together with the silver threads of my hair—and often, very often, must I lay my warm lips against it because it cannot bear its longing."

The white woman held the bound pieces in both hands, and gazed upon them with yearning tenderness, whilst two of the little blue lights hovered near, throwing a beautiful radiance over her face.

"Beside this one I always keep two little flames, because it needs more care than all the others; a poet's heart is so frail a thing; and how much more so a poet that was a lover!"

With the utmost gentleness she laid the heart down and bent towards another.

"This is the heart of a mother who lost all her blessed treasures; see how cruelly wounded it is; but it is the strongest of all, because the strength of a mother's heart is unequalled by any other—and God has a special place awaiting it when the great Day comes."

From heart to heart the snow-maiden moved, with bent head and gentle hands.

The circle of glow-worms round her brow flickered and sparkled like a magic flower.

"This heart," said the snow-maiden, raising a very dark object in her hand, "is black, because it is that of a great sinner; and sometimes the glow that guards it becomes quite small and dim, almost goes out; because the heart suffers greatly of its own wickedness; it was saved because it broke.

"I found it very far off, in a place amongst rocks; and when I tried to raise it, it began to roll away from me, always farther, so that I had to run, to run after it with an anxious feeling that I would not be able to save it. It left traces of blood wherever it passed, so at last I discovered it in a dark hole beside a skull that grimaced at me with a hollow grin: when finally I held it in my warm hand I knew that it was at rest, and I carried it home very slowly.

"Whilst I retraced my steps along the weary way I had come, I sang to it, soft simple songs that children love. As I sang I felt the warm blood trickle through my fingers, and upon the snow I saw that all the drops of blood had run together into the form of a small red cross, which marked upon the whiteness a sign of forgiveness.

"I looked at my hand and noticed that the drops of blood had turned into tears which left no more stain where they fell, but had washed from my fingers all traces of soil. This heart also needs me, but in another way; I always sing to it those simple songs, for it must forget all else except the days when it was at its mother's knee." Stretching her hands across the circle of light the tall vision in the dazzling robe seemed to bless the many waiting throbbing hearts.

"I call this place my garden of expectation! And one day a great joy will arise from it; . . . songs of praise sung by myriads of heavenly voices; . . . and this light is but feeble compared to the light which will shine that day."

Eric was still on his knees; he looked up at that glorious form beside him, and as entranced he watched, her long white hair turned into a soft misty veil that flowed down upon the ice like the mantle of a saint, and the circle of glow-worms had become a halo round the face, that was the face of one of God's own angels.

V

And though blind and deaf for a hundred years I would see her more fair than any poet has sung
FIONA MACLEOD.

ERIC had now left the snow-maiden far behind, had left her there amongst the broken hearts she tended with such gentle hand and deep understanding.

He had gazed his last upon her as she stood in the circle of light all shining and bright; and then, knowing that he must go, he had torn himself away, feeling that otherwise he would not have the strength to continue his road, and part from a being so full of radiance and wonderful beauty.

And now he was wandering in a great forest of fir-trees, his feet skimming quickly over the crackling snow. It was still night around him, but all the trees were lit with millions of candles. Each tree was an enormous Christmas tree. The whole wood was one blaze of light . . . this he knew was the snow-maiden's garden!

It was an astonishing sight; but he fled along; he dared not stay.

As he ran he heard the sound of many wings following him. He lifted his head; in and out through the great branches of the candle-lit pines he saw huge white birds appear and disappear, but so rapidly that he could never distinguish what kind they were.

Now he came out of the forest, and saw a vast frozen sea before him. As he stepped from the shelter of the trees the whole air was filled with white wings. He looked up and saw endless flocks of wild swans; and circling far above them were eagles as white as they, which flew always higher, higher, farther, farther, settling at last upon the blocks of ice that formed forbidding barriers between sea and land.

All these feathered creatures were the companions of the beautiful woman he had left.

He turned, and there, rising above the illuminated forest, far above the clouds, seemingly suspended in the air, was the castle of ice, revealed a last time to his enraptured sight.

He threw out his arms full of longing, as if he too had left his heart within those translucent walls . . . then the heavy snow-laden clouds descended and wiped out the dream like a vision of the night.

VI

Joy rises in me like a summer's morn.
                                    COLERIDGE

It was evening; the sea was calm—so calm that it looked like an enormous mirror into which the sky was reflecting its manifold hues, resembling a crowned woman trying on before her glass various gorgeous robes of glowing colours. Eric Gundian sat at the helm of the boat, his hands folded, gazing before him at the burning horizon; above him the huge rusty sail spread like the giant wing of a bird. The boat moved slowly, and yet it cut steadily through the water, whilst the deep green waves ran along each side like racers—Gundian was waiting . . . he knew not for what, but a great peace was over his soul, and his eyes had a steadfast look of happiness.

The sky was unfurling before him its most precious colours, all the tones of red and gold and orange, reminding him of the palette he had put away.

Now his hands were idle, no doubt, but the artist was still keenly alive, and this beauty and peace seemed part of the very depth of his nature.

Far down within him he knew that his great talent slept, awaiting the day when his hands would be untied to finish his great work.

His hope and trust were simple, and his smile was sweeter than ever.

The red of the sky began now to stain the quiet endless sea—it sank beneath the surface till the whole moving mass was an ocean of flame and light; the little waves that ran along on both sides were like sea-maidens trailing their shining tresses over the water.

Gundian rose and stood at the very extremity of the boat, his slim figure outlined by a circle of light. Then he raised his clear young voice, and sang an old song of his country, a song so strange and sweet, that the sailors behind him took up the chorus and the deep manly voices joined in, forming a long echo to the triumphant notes of their young companion.

He turned round to them, his golden locks thrown back, his beautiful eyes full of dreams and the strength of all his hopes; they had the feeling that with his youth and beauty he was the very incarnation of life and love. Now his voice was softer; the song became a great sigh of longing, like a long-drawn effort towards the boundless, unreachable promises of life.

The old men sank on their knees and the young ones covered their eyes with their hands; each saw before his mind the dreams of his manhood, the loves he had left, the hopes he had buried, the future he longed for or feared.

The glorious colours had paled, only a faint reflection remained; the wind began to fill the sail, the boat seemed to bound forward on its course.

Eric's upright figure had lost its circle of light; his dark form at the helm of the boat was seen now above, now beneath the horizon.

The waves grew in size, and were no longer like slim racers keeping pace with the friendly vessel, but more like great angry beasts longing to consume the frail craft that so confidently rode upon their restless heaving backs.

The sail suddenly filled and expanded ready to burst; and the seamen tightened the cords, being tossed from side to side as they moved about.

Gundian's face was wet with the spray; his bright young eyes peered before him into the growing darkness.

A lantern had been lit and shone far above him like the Star of Bethlehem, flashing on his uncovered head, casting in turn lights and shadows over the fairness of his face. The boat bounded and creaked and groaned; the wind began to howl, frightened gulls flew around the sail with cries of distress, their white wings passing in and out of the gleam of the lantern.

The waves grew greater and greater, beating the sides of the vessel, throwing huge masses of water over the low rail. Eric had to keep a firm grip on the ropes so as not to be hurled into the restless, surging, wailing deep—to him this growing storm was a mighty joy; he revelled in the wind with its many tormented voices; he loved the salt water that dashed in his face, drenched his clothes, and tore at the chain he wore round his neck.

He loved the heaving and sinking of the vessel under him; he loved the weird shrieks of the birds, the flashing of their white wings when they came within the halo,—loved the shimmer of the lantern on the enormous, rolling, always advancing waves.

He trusted the seaman that sailed the ship—trusted the strong boards on which he stood,—above all he trusted with a child's simplicity the great God above.

All through the night the storm howled, and raged, and sobbed; and the brave little craft fought her way through the foaming masses, till the morning slowly overcame the darkness, bringing with the new day a hush that held a promise of peace and rest. Thus did day follow on day, night on night.

Gundian either basked in the sun, or hardened his hands working with the sailors, or sang them sweet songs that melted their hearts, fired their blood, awoke their longings, brought tears to their eyes, or a laugh to their lips. But at times he would also play his little flute; then, all else vanished from his mind, and always, always did the flute hold the same questioning notes that were like the cry of his soul for the unknown vision he was pursuing, that dreams alone allowed him to grasp.

The rough men in the boat looked upon him as a bright being of another sphere. They imagined he brought luck to their voyage, that his presence calmed the storm and had power over the elements, that his wonderful voice and magic flute enchanted the striving, ever-changing winds and waves. They loved him, and were in fear of the day when he would bid them good-bye and withdraw his sunny presence from their lives.

They felt that he was but a bird of passage, that it lay not within their power to keep him for ever amongst them, and each day that they looked on his guileless face and on the light that kindled in his eye, was a gift from on high, a day of blessing and plenty.

Eric could not explain why he remained, neither did he know why all of a sudden, one day of calm and gladness, he felt he must take up again the call of the road that lay before him.

It was on a distant and lonely shore; the boat lay drawn up on the shell-covered beach.

The golden-haired youth looked up into the sky and saw a small bird flying into the limitless distance.

Then Eric knew that he must follow the direction in which the bird had disappeared.

They could not stop him, he had to go. He took his thick stick in his hand, put his flute in his pocket, hung his cloak over his shoulder; then, turning round many a time to wave his cap to the rough companions of yesterday, he walked away into the growing heat of the day.

VII

Yet there was round thee such a dawn of light ne'er seen before.
                                        WOLFE.

THE shore was endless and straight, Eric felt no fatigue ; his face was browned by the wind, the waves, and the sun. His eyes had taken some of the blue of sea and sky. His clothes were soiled, and looked less new than the day he had left King Wanda's palace.

But the chain around his neck glistened in the heat of the noon.

Eric walked and walked, advancing but slowly, because his feet sank into the deep sand as he went.

As usual his heart was full of joy, and it mattered little to him where he went, although no changing beauty of the coast, no small cloud in the sky, no light in the sea passed by unnoticed.

To him each separate beauty was like a picture his soul had conceived.

Now high rocks began to change the aspect of the flat lonely coast, and soon all the young man's activity was needed to climb the obstacles that blocked his way.

From that moment his advance became slower and more painful, he had to draw breath ; more than once he had thrown himself down upon the soft sand, his golden locks hidden amongst the wet pebbles, his heart thumping against his side. But he loved it all, rocks and sea and burning sun ; and each difficulty that arose on the road made him feel but all the happier. A joyful heart is one of God's most precious gifts.

It was late afternoon; and, having climbed over some slippery rocks, Eric reached a quiet little bay, narrow, and rounded by precipitous cliffs on all sides.

There the sea was very silent, very green and transparent, and the flat little waves hardly made a sound as each in turn left a white line of foam along the powdery sand.

Eric lay on his back, his cap drawn over his eyes, his cloak rolled up under his head, a pleasant drowsiness filling his being after the efforts he had made.

Suddenly he sat up with a start, wide awake now, all his senses alert. He had heard something which sounded like the deep tones of a bell, coming from afar off, but distinctly, like a dismal and yet persistent voice, calling . . . calling.

He looked around him full of excitement, keenly interested, and ready for any new adventure.

He rose to his feet and stood, his hand to his ear, listening.

For a moment there was silence, and then again distinctly the sound of a deep-toned bell—and this time he distinguished that the sound came from the rocks that bounded the farther side of the little bay.

Eric felt he must follow that sound; it drew him towards it; he could not resist those deep tones calling, calling. . . . A voice full of warning or invitation? . . .

He could not make out which, neither did he worry his mind about it,—was he not a bird of the air free and joyful, always a song on his lips, loving the sun that shone down upon him, the air that caressed his cheeks, and the good firm earth on which he stood?

The notes of the bell were now louder, now softer; but their tone could not be resisted, and the beautiful youth felt he must follow ; so he began moving towards the spot whence the sound seemed to be coming.

Soon he stood before a high cliff over which long creeping plants were growing, hanging flexible branches covered over and over with some coral-coloured berry, more like long chains of bright beads than a living plant.

This was the only rock on which anything grew, and the shoots took root apparently out of the dark hard stone high above his head. He lifted some of the long trailing branches in both his hands, and as he did so the sound of the bell was distinctly heard, as if quite near.

Eric knelt down and noticed with surprise that there was a large opening in the rock, beneath the coral-coloured plant, like the entry to a cave ; he stooped, carefully avoiding the hanging growth, and advanced gropingly to find himself in a dark tunnel.

The sound of the bell was more and more distinct, the calling more insistent. With crouching gait Eric moved along, feeling his way with his hands; it was quite dark, and the passage was narrow, with damp rough sides, against which he often bruised his fingers.

Now a curious greenish light began to relieve the complete obscurity in which he had been for some minutes, and little by little Eric distinguished in the far distance what was probably the end of the mysterious entry.

The green light became always stronger ; and now our wanderer found himself inside the most marvellous place he had ever seen.

It was a grotto, the walls and domed roof of which had the hue of transparent emeralds ; and all around was green—the rocks, the sand, the deep pool of water at his feet, all radiated rays of liquid green light.

The strip of beach he stood upon was quite shallow, so

that his feet almost touched the deep dark water. In the middle of the tiny lake that filled this wonderful grotto hung a bell, also green and wondrously shining; and although the rest of the water was absolutely calm, strong short waves rose from the centre and hit against the bell, bringing forth the deep boom that had first lured Eric into this magic hall.

Straight across the dark water a narrow bridge was stretched, both sides resting on the tinted sand, passing in the middle quite near to the calling bell.

The bridge was but a yielding plank, a hand's-breadth wide, overgrown with slippery, dripping moss as green as grass on a spring day when the sun shines over it.

The bell gave out weird sounds, sometimes like a cautioning voice warning him against some danger—then again it was full of love and entreaty, containing an endless promise of joy and sweetness.

But Eric was too young and happy to hear within its notes anything but entrancing melodies existing solely to delight his ears.

Unhesitatingly he stepped on to the swaying board, upon which he could only advance by carefully putting one foot before the other, almost like balancing himself on a tight-rope. This gave him great joy, and his merry laugh echoed round the green walls as if he were joking with gay comrades. An immense curiosity was upon him to look at the bell from near, and to see what lay on the other side of the dark lake.

He had the intuition that something still more surprising was hidden not far off.

The slippery plank dipped beneath his weight; he could hardly keep his footing on the slimy moss that clung to it. But Eric was nimble, young, and daring; besides, he could swim like a fish, and was absolutely fearless.

The depth beneath him seemed bottomless; only now and

again his eyes distinguished shadowy forms moving about, but what they were he could not see.

Now he was close to the bell, and the little waves were striking it on all sides, making its tones so varied as to become a bewitching song of penetrating sweetness.

Eric bent his ear down to the bell, which was whispering something to him under cover of the appealing notes,—but he did not understand, he only laughed and stroked the bell, quite heedless of the repeated warning that once again came from the depths of the lake.

He stood up on the quivering footway, and in answer to the old bell's voice he raised his own, clear and ringing, within which lay all the joy and gladness of an untouched heart and an unsoiled life, pure, crystalline, like the voice of an angel.

Stronger and stronger came the floods of melody; all round the green sides the glad notes resounded like a thousand answers, responding to the boundless life-joy that this human voice contained.

Again he bent to the old bell and touched it with both hands; then hurried on over the perilous bridge, eager to reach the other side and to see what lay beyond.

Now he stood on the farther shore; all about him the light streamed green and transparent; but it was not only the green light that shone upon him; another one was penetrating within the dim grotto, showing him a second dark passage beyond; a golden light as if all the rays of the sun had been concentrated into a fiery river.

Eric ran forward like an impetuous child following a butterfly, full of tremendous eagerness for whatever might be waiting there in the middle of that dazzling radiance.

But such beauty met his gaze, such overpowering enchantment, that he stood still completely overcome.

His breath came fast, his eyes stared wide open, enraptured, his artist's soul quivering with ecstasy before what he saw. He was within a hall of purest marble, the walls, and floor, and roof all white and glistening like freshly-fallen snow, upon which myriads of crystals shone, resembling hoar frost on a sunny winter's morn.

In the centre, on a throne, sat a woman whose dress was even whiter than her surroundings. It lay in long straight folds, and the hem was a thick mass of blazing diamonds. It rippled down the steps of the throne, and spread over the spotless floor where the gems flashed in all colours of the rainbow.

The throne was carved out of a gigantic block of pale-green jade that was smooth and polished like ice. The woman's feet rested upon a lion whose skin was as white as the draperies on which he couched. His immense head lay upon his formidable paws, his eyes looked out, with a watchful intentness, beneath his tousled mane. On each side of the throne, fixed into the marble floor, two tall thick tapers burned, whilst the wax ran dripping down their sides like small frozen rivers.

The candles were crowned by flickering blue lights and exhaled a delicious perfume; a vapour rose from them in hazy clouds towards the ceiling, where they hung like a thin mist.

Round throne and tapers garlands of milk-white anemones with golden hearts were wound.

They had shed many of their petals, which lay like snow upon the marble floor.

The woman sat rigid, upright, a mass of fair hair covering her shoulders and streaming down her back.

On her head she wore a thick wreath of the same white anemones fitting closely to her forehead; but the strangest of all was that the woman's eyes were covered with a bandage.

A plain white cloth was bound round her temples beneath the wreath of flowers.

No movement came from the throne; the queenly apparition sat motionless like unto a statue; the light of the candles alone flickered in the still air, and the little bluey mists that arose from them hung over the silent woman's head like a soft veil.

Eric was too entranced by the gorgeous sight to make a single step forward. Yet he longed to tear the bandage from the covered eyes, in the great hope that it might hide the look for which he was ever restlessly searching. Suddenly the beautiful vision rose from her throne, and the great beast at her feet also got up, standing beside her like the guardian of some ancient temple.

Slowly the woman descended the four polished steps, her long robe trailing behind her, sweeping away the fallen leaves of the flowers, the precious gems making a tinkling sound as they hit against the cool green jade.

Her feet were bare, and Gundian noticed, as she placed them by turns on the steps, how marvellous they were.

Slowly she came towards him, both hands outstretched before her, with the searching movement of the blind.

Then Eric, too, advanced with the feeling that he must take one of those groping hands and lead this divine creature wherever she might wish to go.

Now her voice rose soft and bewitching: " Long have I waited thy coming, fair stranger. I have been sitting here on my throne in sadness and silence, because thou hast tarried on the road.

" Thou lovest sky, sea, earth, and sun overmuch, but now that thou hast reached me I shall open unto thee other joys of which thou hast never dreamed.

" Thy way hath been long, and thou hast wasted many a precious day, but let that be of no account now that thou art here," and so saying, with a gentle movement she laid one of her arms about the boy's shoulders and drew him quietly to her over the snowy floor in the direction of her throne.

Eric was speechless, quite unprepared for so warm a reception; but without resistance, as in a trance, he let himself be led by this matchless being of light, and sank down upon the steps of the throne at her feet where the lion had had his place.

And there, his head close against the wondrous woman's knees, he listened in a dreamy transport to the witchery of her voice—not quite conscious of all she was saying, but the sound was so sweet, and the touch of her hand so restful and loving, that all his life throbbed within him in unspeakable delight.

He had entirely forgotten his desire to tear the bandage from her eyes. He felt his will melt beneath her caress and the sound of her voice.

He had no wish left but to sit there for ever, listening and drinking in all the inimitable glory of the place. Now the soft voice was telling him—her face bent down to his, her hair falling in golden waves around him—about all the wonders she was going to show him if he would only remain with her,— of all the riches she would strew before his feet, the music she would play him, the many-tinted flowers she would give him, the costly apparel in which she would clothe him, the variety of sweet-tasting dishes she would set before him to choose from . . . . if he did not leave her!

Eric looked up in surprise; certainly he would not leave her! Why should he go from anything so white, so beautiful, so good, and so fair.

He bent his head and kissed one of the clinging hands that caressed him so softly; oh, without doubt he would stay as long as she wished!

The woman threw back her head and laughed.

Somehow that laugh was the only discord Eric had felt since he was within those walls; but he thought nothing of it, only it was like a little icy drop of water running down between his shoulders—and he wished she would not laugh; far better did he love to feel her soft breath on his cheek, and her gentle fingers passing through his wavy locks.

He rose to his knees on the step at her feet and, seizing both her hands, he begged to be allowed to remove the bandage from her eyes.

But the fair enchantress drew back, disengaging herself from his eager hands.

" For shame ! " she cried, and once more her laugh rang out sharply.

" Who would be so rough ! And wish all the mysteries to be revealed at once ? This cloth over my eyes must remain till I give thee leave to remove it. But much hast thou to learn before that hour strikes.

" It deems me thou art but a reckless youth, understanding but badly how to spend thy riches, little realizing the charm of expectation ! "

And again bending her tantalizing face quite close to his, her lips hidden amongst his curls, she murmured :

" I shall teach thee, oh so many things ; but first of all must I know thy history and why thou art thus wandering aimlessly through the wide, wide world."

Then Eric, still on his knees, his hands pressed against her lap like an anxious child, told her his tale, and how his whole soul was full of the ardent need of finding the face and eyes he wanted for completing his masterpiece. " And perhaps thou hidest behind that cloth the very eyes I have been searching for the wide world over !—that is why my hands are so eager to tear from thy brow what may be masking all my happiness ! "

And then Eric began to plead, his beautiful face flushed and excited, his bright eyes entreating, his body quivering ; indeed, a sight for the gods in all his youthful perfection.

The woman, although her eyes were covered, seemed aware of what was going on, and replied again laughing, " Not yet, not yet !—but give me thy hand and I shall lead thee through the joys I have in store for thee, and at the end thou mayest quite forget what now thou deemest thy only aim in life "; and like tinkling, cold, silver bells the woman's laugh echoed round the snowy vaults.

Fascinated and unresisting our young painter clung to her cool hand, and let himself be drawn away from the white chamber.

He followed her noiseless steps, feeling that wherever she led he would follow, follow, because he had given over his will into those outstretched hands, that had quite taken possession of his heart, and soul, and senses.

VIII

I am restless, I am athirst for far away things.
                                    TAGORE.

ERIC lay at the feet of the enchantress. Days had passed, and from one beauty to another she had been leading him. But her laugh had become always harder, a note of impatience had stolen into the silken tones of her voice.

This youth was in truth but a child, his hands grasping at the sun-rays, plucking the flowers, taking the joys that were offered him, lightly laughing at the birds, sublimely unconscious that perhaps something might be asked of him in return.

Often he begged the one who held him captive to uncover her eyes, explaining that although he was happy in his new surroundings he could not tarry for ever; the open world lay before him through which he was still pursuing the same vision.

But again and again his companion put him off with fresh promises—heaping upon him new joys and pleasures, till he felt weary of so much ease and comfort; there were even times when he had a longing for the dusty roads,—the heat of the sun—the dangers of the dark night—for storm and wind.

At those moments the strange woman seemed to read his thoughts in spite of the bandage over her eyes; and she would redouble her kindness, always having a fresh joy in store for him, something unexpected and enchanting.

Eric lay now, as the lion used to lie, stretched at the feet of the woman he could not leave.

To-day she sat upon a marble bench within a garden where

nearly all the flowers were blue. The garden was small and square, paved with marble; two narrow water channels, lined with peacock-blue tiles, ran crossways through it. In the centre stood a marble well; those who leaned over the side to look into the depths noticed that the water was blue as the sea, and strange voices seemed calling from below with monotonous entreaty.

On all sides high walls encircled the garden, and shady trees spread over the whole enclosure, casting mysterious lights and patterns upon the cool floor.

The flowers were so blue that they also had the colour of the summer sea when the sun beats on it in all his force. Small marble paths ran along between the beds, and each path was bordered by some low-growing fire-coloured flower that glowed with the intensity of a furnace.

Each day the woman was clad in a garment of gorgeous magnificence, each day more splendid than the last; but never again had she been robed in the snowy folds of the first day, which Eric had loved best of all.

Now, as she leaned against the carved bench, her dress seemed woven out of the changing colours of the rainbow. It was golden at the shoulders, turning gradually into green, blue, and violet, always richer in hue, till at the foot it deepened into bright-toned purples upon the dark carpet where Eric rested quite close to her feet.

As always, those little feet were bare, with only thin sandals to protect the soft soles from the hardness of the stone.

Round her forehead lay a thick dark wreath of corn-flowers, beneath which the bandage showed startling white.

Her hands were ceaselessly playing with long chains of sapphires and emeralds. She gathered them into her palms, and let them slip between her fingers, down upon her golden robe, like bright water splashing out of a precious jar.

Around the well, upon low marble seats, were grouped the fairest maidens that earth could give, and they were like unto a wreath of many-shaded flowers.

They all had coronals of blossoms on their heads in the shades of the robes they wore ; and each held a golden harp on which she played tunes that melted heart and soul.

All the maidens turned their eyes towards the beautiful lad who lay among the folds of the woman's dress—but none, oh ! none had the orbs of his dream !

He had searched their faces in turn, and it had been all in vain.

Fair faces they had ; their arms were soft and white ; their long hair trailed on the ground mixing with the petals that had fallen from the wreaths.

The air was heavy with the perfume that came from the flowers, and the sweet tones of the harps sighed amongst the spreading branches of the trees.

But Eric was restless, he felt cramped in this garden of beauty ; resentment began to grow in his heart against this fair being who played with him as a child plays with a toy. She lured him on, yet never did she satisfy the longing of his soul !

Every time that he extended his hand to tear the covering from her eyes, with a word or gesture she changed the current of his thoughts.

When he asked to be shown the road that would take him back whence he had come, the woman would laugh—the laugh he had begun to hate,—and cover his face with soft caresses which seemed to drain all his manhood and leave him without will or power to think.

Within his heart he made plans how he might escape. The sweet perfumes, the melting voices, the endless well-being, the tropical fruit he was ever feasting upon, wearied and sickened him ; and yet he felt he could not leave this bewitching sorceress before he had seen the colour of her eyes.

But somehow, although he wished it with a fevered longing, he also dreaded the disappointment it might bring.

And there he lay in this enchanted garden eating his heart out with the longing for freedom, and yet unable to break through the silken bonds that held him as with chains of iron !

IX

> L'espoir même a des portes closes ;
> Cette terre est pleine de choses
> Dont nous ne voyons qu'un côte.
>   V. Hugo.

Eric was wandering through the maze of gardens, grottos, and domed halls that formed the dwelling of the sorceress. It was night—but a clear night ; almost as light as day because of the radiant moon that lay low in the sky ; she was oppressively near the earth, intruding her wise rays, that had seen all too much, into every corner and hiding-place. Eric hated her indiscretion ; he had hoped to wrap himself in the mantle of the dark so that he might steal away at last.

He could stand no longer the suffocating oppression which had gradually been coming over him. To-night he had slunk away from the luxurious feast his fair jailer had been giving him.

He had left her there, upon her throne of gold, amidst priceless draperies, amongst the garlands of red poppies that had been entwined round the tables at which richly clad, loud-voiced youths were gathered—youths who drank and sang, and whose eyes had a strangely tired look, always straining after some pleasure that seemed to pass them by and leave them with empty outstretched hands.

All had clamoured round that golden throne, pressing near to the queenly figure who sat there in a scarlet robe, her eyes still bandaged beneath the wreath of poppies which was pressed upon her shining tresses.

Her penetrating laugh had sounded clearly above all the din, and she had lifted her hands high in the air throwing the gorgeous-coloured poppy-leaves over their bowed heads; and she had drunk out of a golden goblet which she had held in turns to their thirsting lips.

One of the youths was as young as Eric himself and of marvellous beauty, with eyes like flashing jewels, but which held a look of such intense suffering that Eric could not bear the sight.

This boy had dragged himself on his knees to the steps of the throne, uttering incoherent prayers, the hot tears running down his cheeks; then he had hidden his face within the scarlet folds of her dress and had cried as if his heart would break, whilst the wild woman in red had laughed, laughed, mocking his sorrow with hard words, till all the others had laughed with her.

It was then that Eric had fled, with a mad desire to get out into the cool night and flee as far as he could from all these revels of which his simple soul could not grasp the meaning.

Yet the wonderful woman had dropped some of the poison into his veins, because, in spite of his great desire to escape, he felt a burning regret in his heart at the thought that he was leaving without having seen the woman's eyes. At the same time he almost dreaded to find the face of his dreams behind that white cloth which had become uncanny to him . . . and yet ? . . . why was this burning pain at his heart ? Why had he come here ? Why had he not turned back when the old bell had so persistently warned him ? Suddenly he felt older, wiser, as if years had elapsed since he left the sea-shore and lost his way within this labyrinth so full of beauty and temptation.

He thought he felt once more the soft touch of the woman's hands, that he saw the glowing flower of her lips, the soft yielding figure, the white arms, the rippling fair hair, the tiny feet, and he stood still clasping his hands over his burning eyes.

Why had he not torn the bandage from her brow, and pressed his lips upon that tempting mouth, crushing it beneath his own? Indeed he had been a fool! And no doubt it was thus she considered him, and was now deriding his memory amongst those shameless guests who crowded around her tables; those tables that were bending under the weight of the costly dishes, and where the brilliant poppies were shedding their petals as they faded and drooped amongst hundreds of lighted candles.

Eric groaned in his distress; he longed to go back before that golden throne and tell the beautiful woman that he hated her . . . hated her . . . !

But now he must escape—but why was the moon so bright? Why could he not find his way to the snow-white hall, and from there, over the deep water, past the mysterious well, out into the wide world once more?

Why did his head ache and throb? Why did his throat feel dry with ill-contained sobs? What had come to him? Never had he felt thus.

All the sweet peace of his soul had been replaced by waves of unknown sensations and desires; and beneath it all, that burning pain at his heart, that unsatisfied yearning for something he could not grasp.

The moon flooded everything in a hard, merciless light; he ran from place to place seeking an issue, only to find everywhere blank walls to stop him. He knew that he was losing his head, the blood beat in his temples, his eyes could no more clearly see. . . . With a stifled cry of distress he dropped down, and all became dark around him.

X

For in much wisdom is much grief; and he that increaseth knowledge increaseth sorrow.
                                                              ECCLESIASTES.

AFTER a short time Eric's senses came back; he looked up and saw that he was in a small, very dark chamber. How he got there he did not know, he had never seen the place before. Then he rose to his feet with a start. A curtain had been quietly drawn aside, and he could see now into an inner chamber out of which a faint light shone.

Forgetting all his fear and misery he ran forward, hoping to find an outlet whence he could reach the old moaning bell, and thence escape to liberty under God's great sky, free like a bird once more to wander wherever he would. But the sight he saw riveted his feet to the ground: upon a low narrow couch lay the woman he had learnt to hate. She was stretched motionless, asleep on her back, her wonderful face only faintly discernible—and oh! marvel, her eyes were no longer covered.

All about her seemed wrapped in grey vapours; the soft draperies with which her body was covered were also grey, like finely woven cobwebs.

At each side of her couch, close to her head, stood large jars of tarnished silver, filled with irises the colour of autumn clouds.

At her feet, rigid and unblinking, as if cast out of steel or carved in granite, his eyes gazing into space, was an eagle of unusual size; there he sat in quiet majesty at the feet of this vision of beauty, like a ghost of the mountains that had been turned to stone. A faint haze lay over all, something mysterious and grave-like; nor was it to be discovered whence the light came. There were no windows, no opening anywhere, and yet everything was distinctly visible.

The face of the woman was more perfect than it had ever been. Eric was now bending over it with a feeling of awe and wonder.

Was ever sleeper so still, was ever living face so pale, lips so blanched? Gradually a cold sensation of fear began to creep over the startled youth; he bent lower, his face close to that silent one. He sprang back with a cry of horror . . . beneath the long lashes he saw that the woman was looking at him, and yet . . .

Oh! What was it? What horrible nightmare was this? . . . She was looking, she was staring . . . yes, she was staring with sightless eyes—eyes out of which the light of life had gone for ever! for ever! . . .

Eric sank to his knees and hid his face against the still form, and as he did so he felt something wet upon his cheek, something that was trickling slowly down upon the floor where he knelt, something that was gradually spreading in a dark patch, which widened over the grey folds of the robe. And then Eric saw that within the woman's heart a dagger had been thrust. . . . A dagger within the very centre of her heart.

XI

Over thy creations of beauty there is a mist of tears.
　　　　　　　　　　　　　　　TAGORE.

HIGH and austere in their forsaken silence stood the walls of the great church—God's own sun looked in through the crumbling windows, and God's own sky was its only roof. Many of the columns had fallen, but others stood, erect and rigid, frowning down from their immense height, grey and lonely, like giant trees in winter.

Large heaps of stones lay about the mosaic floor that still showed signs of a beautiful design; statues had fallen from their pedestals and lay in helpless attitudes, their arms broken, their vacant eyes gazing with stony indifference into the sunshine. Sometimes their heads were missing, having rolled away as they fell.

Nature was rapidly doing her work; she was spreading her consoling mantle of verdure and flowers over this crumbling work of art, which human hands had once, long ago, built with pious vows and prayers.

Growths were bursting out of every crevice and crack in rambling confusion. Even the wild plants of the heath beyond had begun to creep into the church, giving the forgotten monument a festive look as if flowers had been strewn everywhere on the floor for some blessed feast-day. In greater masses than any other plant, wild lavender had taken possession of the church, bursting the mosaic floor asunder in a thousand places and pushing its way everywhere, so that over all lay a bluey-grey shimmer like evening mists rising out of a bog.

Through the wide-open portals the desolate land could be seen, stretching as far as the eye could reach, covered with the same dusty blue flower, and quite on the horizon it mixed with the sky, so that it was difficult to discern where the one began and the other ended.

A peculiar stillness lay over everything; it was not easy to imagine that human feet had once crowded towards the now broken altar that shone like a death-cloth as the rays of the sun struck upon the still white stone. The thick carpet of lavender sent out a faint perfume of other days, within which a whole treasure of memories was stowed away . . . forgotten. Peace, peace, peace was over all, the peace of things that are past.

Before the altar, stretched out all his length on the ground amongst the blue of the lavender, lay Eric, his face pressed against the floor, his golden curls matted, his neat clothes soiled and dusty. He lay there, all his young body expressing one long cry of protest against the cruel things he had just learnt.

He had fled and fled, blind instinct guiding his steps, quite ignorant as to how he had found his way out. And then, when he once more saw the great sky over his head, he had rushed unseeingly forward, climbing the rocks, leaving the sea far behind.

On, on, in breathless haste to get away from that silent figure wrapped in grey folds, with the sightless eyes and the dagger within her heart . . . neither did he know how he had reached this desolate place.

He had seen this ruined fane standing grey and forsaken on a waste of blue-grey flowers; he had seen it outlined in magnificent solitude against the clear sky, and a great wish had come over him to take refuge there, in that holy place, after the atmosphere of tragedy and temptation he had just left behind.

What mattered that the place was a ruin, that holy chants and fervent prayers were no more heard within the skeleton walls! It had been God's house, and the weary wanderer needed sanctuary.

Motionless as one asleep or dead he lay.

There was no sound around him except the buzzing of bees amongst the sweet-smelling lavender.

They flitted hither and thither, fetching out of each blossom its treasure of honey and sweetness, whilst tiny blue butterflies danced in their midst in frivolous useless gaiety. All of a sudden a flight of doves came floating out of the summer sky and settled like white sunlit clouds on every window-sill, where they fluttered their wings, filling the whole place with flashes of light, as the sun gleamed on their snowy feathers.

But still Eric lay without movement, his face among the crushed flowers.

The doves cooed and kissed each other; the bees swarmed around, and from somewhere very far overhead a bird sang a glad song, his voice rising shrill and pure into the warm air.

The sun began to slant his rays through the beautiful high windows, lighting up one of the sides of the building with sheets of gold.

He sent his warm beams to kiss the young man's curls, and to caress the white hands that were clasped before him; then one of the rays fell upon a picture that still kept its place above the altar.

At that very moment Eric, for the first time, raised his head—and there, smiling down upon him in angelic pity, was a face of such perfect sweetness, that he felt the hot tears come rushing to his tired eyes.

With folded hands he knelt in a posture of adoration, and

gazed into the wonderful countenance that looked into his. A long cloak of some indescribable shade flowed down, enfolding the Virgin's ethereal limbs. Her hands were outstretched in a gesture of blessing; upon her head she wore a high golden crown, and the sun beat upon it making it shine like real metal; and her eyes, her wonderful eyes, were full of tears. . . . But in her heart. . . . Oh! did he rightly see? or was he dreaming the same awful dream over again? . . . in her heart, too, a dagger had been thrust! Must all hearts be killed? What was this old world teaching him? Was sorrow everywhere? Were those that blessed treated alike with those who poisoned heart and soul?

How ignorant he had been, singing like a bird in the sunshine, understanding nothing, feeling nothing but his own joy to be alive!

Now all seemed changed; pain and temptation, hard words and sweet smiles, had replaced each other in bewildering confusion, and into the heart of this miraculous Mother of God, this most pure of all women they had also thrust a cruel blade —and yet she continued to smile, her fair hands extended to his helpless gropings to understand!

His eyes riveted to the Holy Face, he approached the devastated altar around which the sun-rays had concentrated all their brightness, till the picture of the Virgin was no longer a painting, but a living woman, all light and radiance, Divine pity and love.

The weary wanderer sank on his knees, his hands folded, his head bent on the altar, and as he knelt there murmuring old forgotten prayers of his childhood, real warm tears streamed from the eyes of the holy picture and fell drop by drop on his sunny locks.

And it was like a gentle blessing which held within it a sweet promise of peace and comfort.

XII

THE lavender-covered waste and the gaunt ruins of the church had been left far behind, and our traveller was now ascending the rocky pass of the great rugged mountains that rose high and forbidding above his head. He had felt a longing to climb somewhere very high, with a wish to be as near the blue sky as possible.

Something of the peace that the holy picture had filtered into his heart still remained. Within his clear look there was a dreamy wonder as if he still saw pure visions before him, the warm tears of the Mother of God having consecrated him to a deeper understanding. But there remained a shadow upon his soul from his dark experiences within the dwelling of the sorceress.

He was no more the gay, flitting, singing bird he had been. He strode forward with a more manly tread; something of the boyish eagerness had gone out of his step, some of the sweet confidence had gone from his eyes when they rested on those he met on his way.

When he played on his flute he marvelled at the new tones it had taken; they seemed deeper, sadder, and his voice vibrated less with the joy of living.

Yet the world was still wonderful and full of promise; these rocky mountains had shapes and colours that made his heart rejoice.

In this he was still the same Eric Gundian whom King Wanda had loved: he was without fear, and not even the sight of these treeless giants of stone daunted his wanderer's spirit.

Each night when he slept, no matter where he rested his head, the vision he was following always appeared to him clear, vivid, unchanged—those great solemn eyes that looked into his without ever a droop of the lids. He felt he must cross these enormous heights before he could reach what he was seeking; that as yet his road had been too easy, and that it would be needed of him to make some great effort before he was worthy of attaining his goal.

He looked back in thoughts upon the way he had come, and there seemed to him a great difference between the Eric of yesterday and to-day.

Dense clouds were enfolding the peaks of the mountains and creeping like soft monsters along the sides, filling the deep precipices with damp moving masses which were all coming towards him ready to swallow him up.

Steeper and steeper became the road, the air rarer, whilst the clouds lay thick and impenetrable over all.

Eric toiled on; only seldom could he look down upon what lay beneath because of the vapours that were wrapping themselves around him.

He knew not where he was going, but he stolidly continued his way in spite of the hard rocks and stones that wounded his feet, in spite of the path becoming always more irksome and dangerous.

Often he had but a narrow ledge to walk on, with a chasm on one side, a high wall of rock on the other; and as the clouds lay over everything he was in constant peril of life.

There were moments when a straying sun-ray would break through the clouds, casting a sudden light upon them, transforming them into mother-of-pearl; and sometimes the shaft of light ran straight along the white mist as if a finger of a god were pointing downwards to the dwellings of men.

Then out of the wall of mist a shadow rose and stood before him. It was faintly outlined against the whiteness that was about him, and the shadow was that of a man. And as he looked, full of surprise, another was at his side, and then a third, and these three shades pointed down the road he had been ascending.

Eric turned, and there, behind him, was a whole procession of diaphanous figures all following his footsteps.

They seemed transparent, yet all of them had personality; their faces although blurred and indistinct were full of different expressions.

Some were old and bent, others strong, stalwart, upright. Several of the female figures were young and fair; there were even small children amongst them, and all appeared waiting for him to lead the way.

He moved on, passing the three forms he had first seen, and with a shudder he realized that when he tried to touch them his fingers met nothing but space—his hand passed right through!

And each time he turned his head there they were, all of them, pressing close on his heels, silent, persistent. Truly it was a gruesome company to be wandering with in this wilderness of rocks and clouds.

Eric wondered how long it would last, and if they meant to go with him all the way.

Who were they? And what did they want of him?

Although many of them were beautiful, Eric thought them horrible and uncanny, and kept wondering in what way he could relieve himself of their presence; indeed he had not reckoned with such companions on his road.

Should he turn back ? But if he did he would have to pass them all, and he remembered with a shudder how his hand had gone right through those bodiless shapes when he had tried to touch them, so it was better to go forward instead of retracing his footsteps.

Eric came now to a turn of the path where a great rock jutted out, barring his way in such a fashion that to pass it he would have to put one foot before the other on a ledge so narrow that the sight alone made him feel giddy and faint.

Beneath him gaped the great sea of clouds covering unknown depths he could not penetrate ; but forwards he must go ! Was he not like a hunted animal with this procession of ghosts so remorselessly tracking him ?

He bravely set his face to the dangerous pass, and very carefully, his hands clutching at the rough surface of the rock, he managed to turn the dreaded corner ; as he did so, there, right in the middle of his path, blocking his way, was a very old man.

He sat with head bent, his long grey beard dragging on the ground ; within his clasped hands he grasped a thick stick against which he was leaning.

He looked sad and weary, and yet he was full of quiet dignity ; a surprising figure to meet in a lonely place. His grey clothing hung loosely over his emaciated body, his wide mantle fell in thin folds about him ; on his head he wore a broad-brimmed, weather-beaten hat.

At the young man's exclamation of surprise he raised his head and looked keenly at him, but spoke not a word. Yet this old man was not a spectre like the others, but in verity a living human creature, and for that reason welcome to our lonely wanderer.

"Speak to me," cried Eric. "I am half mad with the longing to hear a human voice. Tell me, if thou canst, who are these silent ones that dog my steps, and make these mountains horrible to me? Fain would I be rid of them!"

He turned to look behind him and there they were, close upon his footsteps, huddled together on the narrow shelf he had just passed; and all of them looked at him with hungry, expectant eyes; and yet through their bodies the rocks could be distinctly seen. It was a grim sight! The old man did not reply, but turned his head towards the silent apparitions and scrutinized them long and earnestly, then a slow smile broke over his face.

At last he spoke:

"Be not hard upon those that are dead, my son; these here find no peace because they did not receive a holy burial, nor were prayers said over their silent hearts; they felt thy coming, so they have arisen from where they lay in waiting, to follow thee. Let thy heart be soft unto them. Their presence around thee speaks in thy favour, for they try to follow only those whose conscience is without stain, for those alone can help them whose lives have been pure."

"Who are they?" asked the young man, and the old one answered:

"They are the restless souls of those who died here amongst the mountains. They all had hopes in their hearts when they started, and dreams or ambitions; each thought himself strong enough to scale these cruel heights, but they dropped down on the way; few, very few, ever reach the top. They lose courage or weary and try to turn back; but it is difficult to go back for those who have started on these paths that lead so high."

"Tell me, O wise man," cried the youth, "what mountains are these, and why did I feel that I must try to ascend them?"

"They are called the mountains of Life, my son. For some they bear also the name of the mountains of Temptation; for others they mean Toil; for others Trouble; for some they are named Redemption, and for the fewest they are called the mountains of Attainment."

"For me what shall they be called, my father?"

"That remains to be seen, my boy," responded the solemn voice.

"Tarry awhile beside me and I shall tell thee a few things that may be of use to thee. Thy fair face pleases me, and I wish thee well. But I am old, and my voice has no more the force as of a river in spring-time when the snows have melted; it is more like a sluggish stream over which a thick sheet of ice has been laid. But sit thee down close by me that I need not raise it overmuch."

So saying he drew his cloak away, making room for Eric on the rock where he was resting. The waiting shapes had become fainter, and were like torn pieces of mist that had caught upon the rocks.

"But before all else, I pray thee, tell me," said Eric, "why thou sayest these shadows have awaited my coming; and why thou dost not thyself lead them to peace? Thou who art so wise?"

The venerable face turned to the young one with a sad smile, and the old solemn voice answered in a low tone, "To be wise is not the same as to be good. Long ago, in the days of my youth, and later also in the years of my manhood, I was a great sinner, and many a dark unavowed act have I committed. But wise I always was, and even magic have I understood.

"There comes a time, my son, when the heart longs for peace; the white peace of solitude. Amongst men it could never be found, so I came up here; but that was only after my head had bent beneath the snow of age, after I had tasted all fruits both bitter and sweet; and this I tell thee: few are worth the eating. Yet thou shalt also eat of many; but have a care, I pray thee, and grasp not those that were best left untouched; and yet? and yet?

"When I look back I know it all had some meaning behind it—something that was but a link of one long chain, and the chain is so long that the links are but of small importance, although each link deems itself the one which holds all the chain together; and it is better it should be so, because the long chain needs each separate link. My talk is dark to thee," added the old man, laying his hand on Eric's.

"Forgive an old man whose thoughts ramble along; seest thou, up here in this wild solitude amongst the clouds and eagles, one learns to look down upon things and to realize their value; but it is useless to begin such knowledge too soon, for we, the weary ones, need all thy joy, all thy careless happiness, we need thy efforts, thy hopes, thy dreams, thy tears; none are wasted; they all go to make one great whole! Life is long and yet it is short, and many roads there are, but they all, without exception, lead to the same end. I am very near that end now; some reach it sooner than I. I know not what thou seekest, but all men are running after the same thing, though they call it by different names, not knowing that they can grasp but its shadow, because the thing itself is God's.

"I have given it a name. I call it Happiness; but truly this I can tell thee: men know not when they have it . . . they see it before them, and then they turn round and they see it far behind . . . but whilst it is theirs they are blind. Dark are my words to thee, but I love thee the more, because I read within thy eyes that all I am saying is without sense to thee, dear beginner of Life."

"But thou hast not told me," queried Eric, "why these phantoms hope to find salvation through me, and why with thy great wisdom thou canst do less for them than I with my foolish youth?"

Sadly the old man replied:

"Because, my son, youth and innocence have a strength that all the wisdom from over the seven seas cannot equal. Indeed, we who have lived and now look back, are far more willing to stretch out our hands in help; our hearts are larger, our patience greater, our understanding deeper; but it has thus been decreed that all this cannot be weighed against one little drop of thy pure innocence or of the faith thou hast, that removeth mountains."

The old head bowed itself over the clasped hands, and on the long grey locks lay a mist that was silvery and lustreless, as if some one had breathed over a mirror.

The sad, tired eyes gazed with a far-off look into space, following forgotten visions of long ago.

There was a deep silence which the young man did not try to break. He bowed in awe before this gaunt old figure, and longed to hear more, to drink in the wise words that fell from his lips.

Although many were quite incomprehensible to him, his instinct told him that he could learn much wisdom if he listened with all his soul. Strange it was that such a man should call himself a sinner when such a delightful peace filled Eric's whole being as he sat there close beside him.

The old man turned his head and looked into the young man's eyes.

"Fair thou art in thy glorious untouched youth. I did not hope to look again on so good a sight. I wish I could give thee some of my wisdom to keep thee from harm, but a loving, pure heart is also a shield, perhaps even better than any I could give thee; and yet when old age lifts its eyes to look upon youth, and sees it beautiful, a prayer comes to its lips that it may remain thus unsoiled for ever!

"Thou must go forth without fear; and have patience, dear youth, with those quiet followers of thine. If thou art strong enough thou mayest lead them to peace; for this I must tell thee: thy way will be hard and long till thou reachest the end which is thy desire; but by the love of my snowy hair I entreat thee climb to the highest summit, let not thy soul be satisfied till thou hast scaled the last, steepest peak.

"There may be easier roads, but take them not; others may tempt thee from thy giddy path, but listen not to their talk. I shall put all my faith in thee, and I will not that thou disappoint me. Before I die, I want to know that one has reached the greatest height."

"But tell me," cried the youth, "will I find at the end that for which I am seeking, which I am wandering after all the world over?"

"That I cannot answer thee now, my son," replied his companion. "Come with me to my dwelling; I shall gaze into my magic stone and perchance I shall be able to tell thee. Give me thy hand, for I am weary; we have not far to go, and it will be sweet to me to lean upon thy youth."

With great care and solicitude Eric helped the feeble old hermit to his feet, and following the gentle pressure of his hand, he let himself be directed to the mouth of a dark cave, hewn out of the rock, close to where they had been sitting.

"What a lonely place to live in!" cried the young man. "In truth it is like an eagle's nest hung on the very edge of the precipice!"

"It is a good dwelling for me, who only want to look backwards and not forwards," said the old man.

"Here I live in peace away from the clamouring of the

crowd; I live with the thought of what has been, and what was evil drops away from what was good.

"I remember far more clearly the sun that shone than the days that were dark. I see faces I loved, and those I hated have no more power over me. Even strange it seems that once I could hate; yet well do I remember how I loved; for this also shalt thou learn: that Love is the beginning and end of all things.

"Love is the key that opens every door. Love is the answer to all questions. Love is the very centre of the heart of the universe. Love is the voice of God, the punishment and the recompense He gives to His people.

"Love carries the heart to the verge of the unknown. In Love all is contained: joy and pain, hope and despair, the night and the day; what was, what is, and what shall be . . . but again my tongue wanders away with me, soon thou shalt weary of my talk.

"Look about thee and tell me if my dwelling is to thy liking."

The cave in which they stood was dark; but when Eric's eyes had got accustomed to the dimness he saw that indeed it was but a poor abode.

His host lit a small ancient oil lamp which spread a feeble light around. He placed it upon a table hewn out of the root of a tree, and sat heavily down on a stool near by, resting his head in his hand, his still keen eyes following the young man's movements as he looked about him.

The cave was not large, and the sides were of bare stone. A cavity had been cut out at the farther end where a few rough skins were spread, and that was the bed, indeed more like a grave than a resting-place.

In one of the corners there was a rude hearth with a few old pots; opposite was a shelf bending beneath the weight of many old volumes bound in shabby leather; a tiny aperture gave a very faint light somewhere near the roof, otherwise the door was the only opening; it was shut by a thick woollen curtain hung on a string.

Against one of the walls stood a large wooden chest covered with an old shawl, once of fine bright texture, now so mellowed by age that its curious design was hardly discernible; a few low stools and a big heavy table completed the whole furnishing of this primitive dwelling.

"Well," asked the hermit, "what sayest thou to my sumptuous apartment?"

Smiling down upon his host Eric rejoined:

"Somewhat gloomy it seems to me—and too near the edge of the precipice on dark nights. In very truth the thought makes me shudder, that if one had not a care one could step from the door over the brink!"

The old man laughed softly, but with the sound of some one who for many a year had no more been accustomed to mirth.

"Come and sit thee by me, for I still have much to tell thee. Take yonder stool, bring it close to my side that I need not raise my tired old voice."

As Eric sat down he saw that two covered objects lay upon the table. The hermit stretched out his trembling hand and drew the smaller of the two towards him, raising the dark cloth that covered it.

As he did so, a round ball, cut out of a stone the colour of smouldering ashes, became visible; it was resting on a small three-legged stand carved in old ivory.

"I shall now look into this magic ball to see thy future, dear wanderer. Give me thy hand whilst I concentrate my mind upon the polished surface; thou must think with all thy might of that which is thy greatest desire, and thou must not speak or the charm will be broken."

Eric laid his hand confidently within the dry wrinkled palm, and remained silent, as he had been bid, his face near to that of the old man, his fair locks resting against the silvery ones.

With breathless intensity he watched the magic ball, and saw with wonder how it began to glow as if a fire were burning inside.

The curious light became always more intense till the ball was one burning flame upon which he could hardly keep his eyes.

He felt an unwonted drowsiness come over him, but with all his might he kept his mind fixed upon the eyes of his dream, and then out of the silence came the voice of his companion, inexplicably changed and musical, like far-off bells.

"I see a great picture on a wall—in the middle of which there sits a woman on a throne, the woman has no face. . . . I see eager questioning all around thee, but there are tears in thy eyes. . . . I see a long road on which thou art wandering mostly in the brilliant sunshine, but sometimes it is the moon that lights thy way. Thy tears have dried, but thou knowest not where thou goest and thou singest like a bird. Many other faces cross thy road and mostly they smile on thee. . . .

"But somewhere there is a shadow that falls over thy path and thou art afraid—something there is that thou dost not understand and that contains sore temptations for thee . . . then. . . . Yes, if I rightly see . . . there is blood, it drips slowly to the ground, but thy own hands are without stain, yet thou art full of fear and fleest as quickly as thou canst.

"Then again there is sunshine, and round thee all is blue, the sky as well as the ground—then once more there are tears, warm and wet, but this time they are not thine. . . . And now thou wanderest where the air is rarer and thy breath comes in gasps—thou mountest ever higher and higher . . . there comes a moment's rest and again thou art wandering, and always thy road is steeper and thy step more weary. . . . All around thee there are shapes that make thee afraid.

"And now I hear the voice of a child crying, crying . . . again a shadow falls over thee . . . this time like to the shadow of death."

The chanting voice paused and the grey head bent closer down upon the fiery ball; the pressure upon the young man's hand became an iron grip. Drops of perspiration stood upon the wrinkled brow as if an enormous effort were being made. Then the voice spoke again:

"What I now see is a long road through a country of sunshine and riches—it is evening, sweet music rises in the air, a haze of dust lies over the horizon; then all I see, at the end, is a face of wonderful sweetness, yet sad and full of yearning—and I see two eyes . . . strange and wonderful, and somehow thy heart is at peace. . . . That is all."

The voice had ceased; the grip upon the young man's hand had relaxed, a heavy silence lay over them.

The glow in the magic ball died down till only the smouldering colour remained. Then Eric spoke like one in a dream:

"Thou sawest the eyes! deep, grey, unblinking, sad, and yearning? So I shall reach them in the end! Canst thou not tell me whose they are?"

The old man's head had fallen on his breast as if overcome by fatigue; now he raised it very slowly and looked long and lovingly at the young eager face.

"Nay! that I cannot tell thee, but this I know: Happiness cometh not there where we seek it; it cometh like a breath out of the unknown, and then the heart is glad and a great light is spread over all that our eyes rest upon. Then we are full of strength and courage, and each man is our friend.

"But the thing we clasp to our heart is never ours to keep, for thus it is in this world. Joy and pain lie so close side by side that there seems no line to cross between the two—and yet when crossed. . . . Well, my son, I shall show thee what no other eye but mine own has ever looked upon ; it is all that remains to me of what was on the other side of the line. . . ."

The trembling hand removed the cover from the second object that lay on the table, and there, revealed to Eric's astonished gaze, was a face the like of which he had never seen before.

It lay, the head thrown back, the eyes closed, the lips slightly parted as if asking for a last caress.

The hair waved away from the delicate, somewhat sunken temples, forming the pillow on which it rested.

A calm expression of peace lay over the angelically pure features that had the soft whiteness of ivory.

There was no colour save a faint tint of pink on the beseeching mouth. Yes, it was peace that was the principal expression of that face, and yet there was also a sad yearning in it, as if the closed eyes longed to raise their lids a last time to look upon a face they loved. . . .

The old man's head now lay on the hard table upon his outstretched arms ; he was overwhelmed by some tremendous emotion, unable to look at those silent features.

The youth knew not what force moved him, but he knelt down beside the emaciated old figure and, taking it into his strong young arms, he drew the bowed head towards him, and held it long against his heart in a silent embrace.

After a while both looked up and the grey hermit pressed one of his shaking hands on the young man's head; the other he laid with a caressing movement against the marble face.

" I have worked at this with the last strength of my feeble old hands. And each day for many years I laboured to create the fairness of this face which I loved, but which never was mine !

"I will not weary thee with the story of my life; it is dark and ugly, but this thou shalt know: I loved her, and she gave me all the passion of her pure heart. She knew not who I was, and when she found it out she could not bear the truth, so she searched a cold grave in the deep, dark floods. Thus she lay when last I looked upon her; the vision burnt itself deep into my brain for ever. For long, long years after she had crossed my path I continued to live a wicked life, full of dark deeds, full of treachery, keeping faith with none.

"But when, old and bent, I came to these solitudes her face alone was always with me. Then I began to carve upon the snowy marble the features I had loved the most in this world.

"Day by day I toiled, for my fingers were stiff and trembling, but I felt I could not die before I had completed this work of love. I felt that if I could conjure into life the marvel of her face as it was that day when they took her out of the cruel water and laid her, for ever silent, before me, her murderer, I would find forgiveness before that God I had always mocked but had learnt to believe in here in this vast solitude so near His sky!

"It is but a short while ago that I completed my work; thou seest thyself how surpassing fair it is, and since that day peace at last seems to be spreading very slowly over my soul. . . ."

The old man paused, then drawing the youth quite near to him, he took his head in both his hands, bent it gently back, saying in a solemn voice:

"Remember the words of a very old man, who has known all of pain and joy, who also has lived through the hell of remorse though it came too late . . . too late. . . . Mayest thou never learn how sad is the word: Too late! Go thy way, my son. Search for the treasure thou dreamest of, and when it is thine hold it fast. It may come to thee in quite unexpected form—at first even thou mayest not realize that thou art so near ; it may not come in splendid raiment with a crown on its head, but keep thy heart open as well as thy eyes ; turn not away from the humblest call, never leave undone a deed of love.

"I, in my solitude, well know what it is to bitterly regret. All the wisdom I have acquired is but ashes to me because never did I understand how to use my riches,—I cherished what was of brass, and what was pure gold, in my vanity, I trampled underfoot. Thou hast within thee something that makes me believe thou art of those who win! Now I have said enough, and thou must continue thy road; but that thou shouldst not forget the grey hermit of the hills, I have for thee a gift, which, in the days of my youth, was my most trusted friend. In thy hands it will have greater power than ever it had in mine."

So saying the old man rose, went to the bed, and drew something out of the dark. When he came back he held within his hand a shining sword.

"This sword have I loved in the pride of my youth, and even now, in my bitter old age, it was ever at my side. Whilst I worked at the cold, hard marble, it lay on the table near my hand ; it alone felt my hot tears of gratitude on the day I had completed my work.

"A legend is attached to it: it is said that if carried by hands that are clean of all sin it has unknown powers that reveal themselves in time of need. It may be true . . ." the old man bowed his head. . . . "But my hands . . . were never clean . . . so no miracle shone on my road.

"To me it was simply a good strong sword which I used in my own defence. I used it, too, against my country's foes, and many an evening has it dripped with blood. Gird it round thy waist and go forth with my blessing. I know not if the blessing of a man such as I hath worth in the eyes of God; nevertheless it comes from the deepest depths of my weary soul, and may it follow thee wherever thou goest and help thee to win."

Eric bent his knee, and the hermit laid both his hands on his golden locks, lingering tenderly over them as if loath to take his fingers away.

" One more gift have I for thee, my son, for I know the peril and loneliness of thy road. Here inside this box "—and he drew a small casket from his breast—" thou shalt find some tablets I once learnt to make, and which possess marvellous power to keep the traveller alive when he can find no food on his way; one of these alone is as much as a feast at the table of a king. Neither is this their only magic; for he who tastes of them to him is given command over all languages spoken under the sun."

" But am I not taking thy daily bread from thee ? " cried the young man, as he sprang to his feet.

" Be without fear, dear youth; my days are numbered, and enough remains to me to keep my tired old body alive, as long as God still desires me to be of this earth. Go in peace, and have a kindly thought for the old sinner whose last joy has been to look into thy sunny eyes ! "

He led Eric to the door of the cave, and pulling the curtain aside, gave a strange, shrill whistle.

As he did so there was a fluttering of wings, and somewhere out of the clouds a milk-white falcon swooped down to his hand.

" This bird of mine will show thee the road. Follow him without faltering, even if he seem to lead thee where no foot can climb. Be of good cheer, may God be with thee ! "

Eric bowed his head, kissed the kind old hand, and then

turned his face towards the lonely path he had to follow, the hawk flying before him like a white banner floating in the wind.

The old man stood on his threshold casting longing looks after the retreating form. An expression of intense sadness and resignation came over his furrowed countenance; slowly, with all the fatigue of nearly a century's living heavy upon him, he went back into his dark abode. There he stood for a long while beside the rustic table contemplating the pale marble face, and all his soul was in his eyes. The flickering light played on the exquisite visage, throwing over it a living warmth, so that the eyelids appeared to quiver as if they were trying to open once more.

Slowly and painfully the aged recluse bent down till his faded lips rested on the pure brow, the icy coldness of the stone penetrating through all his veins—then with a reluctant movement he laid the dark cloth over that vision of beauty, hiding it out of sight; and it was like the lid of a coffin being shut over the face of the dead.

XIII

> And a strange song I have heard
> By a shadowy stream,
> And the singing of a snow-white bird
> On the Hills of Dream
> > FIONA MACLEOD.

THE white wings of the bird could be seen far overhead. Eric looked up and understood that at whatever cost he must scale those heights towards which it flew. Such had been the decree of the kind old philosopher.

Firm was his resolution to obey him in everything, because never before had human being spoken thus unto him.

Only one fact his mind refused to grasp : how could such a man be a sinner ? He thought of the gentle, venerable face, of his wise and beautiful sayings ; and dear to his memory was the sound of his voice. His feelings towards the silent ghosts, that still followed him, were quite changed, for the words of the master were ever in his mind.

He felt now a kindly interest in their welfare, and hoped that strength would be given him to lead them to peace. The clouds lay no longer so dense over his road. He could advance with greater rapidity.

Always steeper grew the way, and always higher flew the bird ; often its white plumes were lost amongst the floating mist.

Eric was full of courage and hope ; whilst he walked he kept thinking of all he had heard. Tears came to his eyes at the remembrance of the silvery head lying so close to the cold hard marble which made no response, the face in its immaculate fairness so serenely unconscious of all the feeling its beauty called forth.

Within the stern silence of that pale stone lay a punishment far greater than human justice could inflict.

Night was coming on, but Eric still advanced with undaunted step, ignoring the fatigue that was again making itself felt through all his supple limbs.

The sword at his side gave him a companionable feeling; his eyes rested upon it with pride, admiring the beautiful hilt that was carved out of a single piece of crystal in the form of a cross. In the centre had been set a large emerald the colour of a deep forest pool, transparent and dark, evoking a feeling of rest amongst glorious solitudes where the foot of man but seldom passes.

The blade was as bright as silver, and flashed like a search-light when Eric drew it from its sheath. He did so more than once, feeling its edge, with the joy of a child over a new toy.

Never had he possessed so manly an arm, and his pleasure knew no bounds.

Always darker grew the night, more perilous the path. Our valiant wanderer was now obliged to feel the way with his hands, and began to think about where he could lay himself down to rest. It was useless to press onward without seeing where he was going—useless to risk making a false step that might perhaps cost him his life by hurling him into the chasm that yawned at his side.

His only fear was to lose sight of his feathered companion; it would be almost impossible to find it again in this desert of rocks. He stood still to think what he had better do, when out of the darkness, quite close before him, he saw the flash of white wings.

He sprang forward in pursuit, regardless of the danger

that gaped around him ; and after a moment he found himself on a broad ledge under the protection of a jutting rock. There, just discernible, in the dense obscurity sat the white falcon, motionless, at rest, giving the sign that here they should make a halt.

The great bird turned its head towards the youth, and as it did so something resembling a tiny light gleamed on its breast.

Eric approached it cautiously for fear of frightening it away, but the beautiful creature showed no signs of alarm, and let him lay his hand on its head.

Then Eric saw that around the strange bird's neck a tiny chain was clasped, from which hung a diamond of prodigious size ; it radiated a strong bluish light much like that of a shimmering star. Here in this vast wilderness of unknown perils the little light shone brightly like unto a kindly eye that had been placed there to watch over him during the night.

With a sensation of comfort Eric laid himself down close to the quiet guardian, wrapping himself up warmly in the folds of his cloak, for the night was cold.

Indeed the rocks made but a hard and unfriendly bed, but Eric was young, and weary was his body, so it was not long before sleep came down and carried him off into the land of dreams.

Upon the rock near his head sat the motionless, wakeful bird of prey, staring with unblinking eyes into the dark. The whiteness of its feathers was faintly visible, and the blue diamond burned steadily like the lamp of a lighthouse seen from far over the sea.

Now there was a faint movement about the sleeping boy and that silent watcher of the Hills.

A circle of mist seemed to be settling around them, like a giant wreath of grey poppies ; but it was not the vapours of the night that were forming a ring round the man and the bird—it was the bodiless army of following ghosts; and there they sat a quiet company, forms out of another world, awaiting in mournful silence that this frail human being should arise to lead them over perilous ways to the height that would be their salvation.

XIV

> Far off I hear the strain
> Of infinite sweet pain,
> That floats along lonely phantom land.
>
> FIONA MACLEOD.

ERIC had not slept many hours before he awoke with a start. All was pitch-black around him, only the form of the white hawk was outlined against the darkness, whilst the precious stone on its neck shone in lonely magnificence.

Eric sat up wondering what had torn him so suddenly out of his restful slumbers; he felt rather stiff from the hardness of his stony couch, so sprang to his feet and stood erect, listening, awaiting any danger that might threaten him out of the unknown. And then, suddenly, a wailing cry broke out of the stillness; it rose like a frightened sob into the air and rang through the night with a sound so full of terrible loneliness that it made the heart stand still.

The bird stretched its neck, its wings expanded ready to take flight, the light of the diamond twinkling on its breast.

Eric waited, trembling with expectancy; there was something weird and heartrending about that helpless cry out of this boundless solitude; again the dismal sound was heard, distinct and piercing like the terrified voice of a very small child in an agony of fear.

Eric could bear it no longer, and sprang in the direction whence the sound came.

At that moment his beautiful winged companion rose in

the air, circling close around the path he was on, so that the jewel flashed in moving patterns like a small lantern being swung over his head.

Eric followed the tiny light, grateful for that dwarf spot of brightness, which shone in the thick darkness that hemmed him in on all sides. Many a time he stumbled over the stones that obstructed his road, often bruising his hands and knees, sometimes falling all his length, but always desperately aware how perilous and uncertain was this search in the impenetrable night.

Now the wonderful bird paused in its flight, and Eric saw the small light, suspended in the air, hovering over one particular spot: he groped about, his hands feeling everywhere—what was he to find? All at once, close above his head the pitiful voice was again heard, but this time quite near. With breathless anxiety Eric scaled the rock, quite unable to see where he was going; but his hands were always outstretched, carefully seeking about him, and now his fingers suddenly came in contact with something soft and warm!

With gentle precautions the young man drew the heavy object towards him, balancing himself with surprising agility upon the narrow ledge . . . and there, in his arms, against his cheek he felt the soft face of a little child! . . . Yes, a little child, whose pitiful moan rose to the sky like a soul in distress. Clasping the small body close to his breast, the young man with an almost superhuman effort hoisted himself on to a shelf-like rock he had felt near by, and there he sat himself down with his precious bundle in his arms.

As he did so the falcon swooped out of the air on to his shoulder, so that the light of the gem could just fall upon the pale small face that looked up into his.

Such a sweet little face, out of which two frightened eyes stared up at him in speechless anxiety. Miserable rags alone covered the thin body that was shivering with cold.

Eric drew his cloak close around the trembling form and held it tight against him, whilst with kindly words he tried to calm its ceaseless whimper.

Long he sat thus in this vast black solitude, whilst upon his shoulder the friendly bird kept watch over the two forlorn young creatures who had been so strangely brought together in these lonely hills.

Eric's eyes closed, and the child too, feeling comforted, was quiet now, its head hidden against the kind heart that had been its saviour.

Probably both slept, because when Eric next looked up there was a faint red streak in the sky; the darkness of the night was slowly lifting.

The little girl was huddled up close in his arms slumbering sweetly.

Near by on a block of granite the beautiful hawk sat like a watchful guardian—his keen ever-open eyes fixed in an unblinking stare upon the rising sun.

XV

SEVERAL days later Eric could have been seen advancing over the frozen ground holding a small child's hand safely clasped in his own. He had wandered and wandered, climbing always higher, never giving way, no matter how overpowering his fatigue. For ever ringing in his ears was the sound of the solitary man's voice begging that he should not disappoint him by turning back, urging him to have courage to go always forward till he had climbed the highest peak!—not to be afraid, because he believed Eric to be of those who win. Ah! but would he win? Would he ever reach the top of those lonely heights? would he ever look down upon the other side? At first the thought of having a companion on his arduous way was a comfort to him. The child's face was sweet, its eyes looked up into his with a trust and confidence that gladdened his spirit.

But soon he understood how much more slowly he could advance; how he had to redouble his efforts at every step; how much more often he had to rest because of the toddling feet at his side, and often, very often the child's head pressed against his cheek; he carried it for many weary miles, till his powers were nearly spent.

From whence the child came, whose it was, how it had been lost here amongst these drear solitudes Eric could not get it to relate.

When he pressed it with questions it would only cry helplessly, and point always before it, as if longing to reach the most giddy heights.

The only words it seemed to know were the strange little cry of : " Up, up," or " Over there, over there," and persistently with its tiny hand it pointed to the most distant horizons ; and then a feverish shine of expectancy would light its eyes and a flush come over its wan little cheeks.

He loved the lonely wee maid, but a frightful apprehension was pressing at his heart—would he be strong enough to save them both ?

The magic tablets out of the old man's box were diminishing day by day. He wondered how far he still must go before he had scaled the last rock.

The child was frail and delicate : its feet were bare, the wretched dress it wore hung in discoloured rags round its thin body. Dark curls clustered round a face of angelic beauty, pale and haggard though it was, out of which the eyes looked like those of a frightened gazelle.

With touching gratitude the little creature clung to this man who had saved it in its dire distress, and often Eric would feel the pressure of its warm lips against his hand as they trudged on side by side.

Their weary feet were now carrying them across the precipitous incline of a great mountain, the most mighty of all the range, the one whose summit bore the highest peak, the one Eric had singled out as the ultimate object of his steep ascent. Their way lay across wide-spreading mountain meadows, now covered with a white sheet of snow and frost ; far ahead lay a dark forest of pine which they would have to traverse before reaching the final ridges beyond.

Always close upon his heels followed the silent army of ghosts, and the higher their leader climbed the more hopeful was the look of their eyes ; it almost seemed that their bodies were becoming less transparent, that each separate form was losing something of its mist-like frailty.

The little maiden was not afraid of them, and often, when weariness had obliged her and her companion to rest, she would stretch out both small arms in their direction, inviting them to share her repose. And then it would happen that out of that sad troop of followers other arms—perhaps the empty arms of what had once been a mother—would answer with the same yearning gesture of love, and yet all the distance of two worlds lay between them, and the bridge had not yet been built over which they could meet !

The little one loved to hear Eric play on his flute ; so even when most overpowered with fatigue, his breath coming in gasps, he would take it from his pocket and try to call from it its sweetest notes. But often he would have to lay it down, his lips were too dry, his hand shaking overmuch.

The continual strain upon his youthful body was telling at last, and often he had to cover his eyes with his hands, because a sudden dizziness would overtake him.

He was in such fear that the mysterious tablets in the small box would come to an end that he ate of them but sparingly, giving his companion the larger share.

Eric had been accustomed to live in plenty ; had he not been the favourite of a king ? And now a precious life had been given unexpectedly into his hands—the bright singing bird, the gay flitting butterfly had to learn to live for another ! His face had lost its roundness, the smile was still bright and sunny, but his eyes wore an anxious look that seemed for ever searching the distance. A new feeling of softness had stolen into his heart; those two slender arms, that tiny confiding hand within his own, those pattering feet beside him, awoke within his soul sensations of which he had never even dreamed.

He felt that gladly would he suffer any pain, gladly lay down his life, if this sweet being that trusted in him could but remain unharmed.

Once on a steep pass she had fallen, bruising her delicate feet and cutting her face. He had held her then in his arms as a mother would have done, and an indescribable feeling of tenderness had flooded his heart, whilst her warm tears had wetted his cheek as he pressed her close to him. The sensation of that soft little body clasped against his own during the cold nights they had slept side by side, his cloak covering them both, was to him like treading on Holy ground! And now with growing apprehension he saw the great forest opening its sombre paths before him.

The falcon flew leading the way, its white plumage showing like some gigantic flower against the dark branches.

What secret terrors were hidden within that green solitude? How would they find their way out? Indeed helpless did he feel; how could he protect this frail child against the cold that was always becoming more biting, searching its way under their skin trying to freeze their blood!

Onwards! onwards! it was no good standing still; but the effort was greater with every step.

Now the green forest had received them within its thickness; immense trees looked down upon them waving their branches, whispering together, astonished at the sight of two such defenceless travellers venturing themselves within their dreaded obscurity.

The snow lay thick on the ground, always deeper the higher they climbed, and there came a moment when the little girl, clinging to her kind companion, cried bitterly, declaring that she could go no farther.

In despair Eric looked around him—on all sides the awful solitude shut him in; rows on rows of giants frowned down upon his sorry plight, the wind rustled through their branches that looked like monstrous arms gesticulating in angry discussions over the heads of these two forlorn human beings. To Eric they suddenly appeared like enemies come together from all parts of the world to plan his destruction.

Each tree was a living creature threatening him, trying to stop him, to turn him back ! He clenched his teeth : he would not go back ! He would not give up ! He would not allow fear to fill his soul ! Was he not to be of those who win ? Had not the hermit believed in his courage ? and his silent followers had they not put all their trust in his strength ?

There they stood, fantastic forms hovering on the verge of Eternity, faintly discernible against the trunks of the trees, their haunted eyes turned towards him, their transparent bodies all bending his way in hushed expectation.

The wind came down in howling gusts, stirring up the withered needles that lay on the snow, bending the proud trees before its ruthless violence, dashing powdery clouds over the trembling child ; then rushing in shrieking hordes through the sombre pines so that their boughs clashed together like an angry mob. Night was coming on ; all around Eric could see nothing but trees, trees—an army of Titans allied against him to hinder him reaching his goal. To add to the horror of his pitiful situation, he thought he heard from afar the howling of wolves, and that he saw creeping forms slinking amongst the thickening shadows.

Calling upon all his courage, he bent down and gathered the exhausted child into his arms, wrapping the folds of his cloak tightly round her shuddering limbs ; and thus weighted he struggled on, his breath coming in gasps, his pulses beating, a mist before his eyes.

He toiled through the snow, up, up, winding his way between the trunks of the hostile trees—often stumbling—hitting his weary feet against broken twigs—straining with a feeling that his veins would burst, so great was his exertion.

But he would not give way! He would not lay down his precious burden before he could find some cover for the night! To rest there upon that bed of snow would be certain death; his weariness was such, he knew if once he fell it would be to rise no more—he would hide his head in that icy shroud dragging down the precious life with his, to never, never move again.

On—on . . . but was the child of lead? Why had his arms become so weak? Why were dark vapours floating before his eyes? . . . Why had he a beating heart in each tingling nerve of his aching body? Why did his tongue cleave to the roof of his mouth, whilst fire seemed to course down his throat? And now a great darkness suddenly wiped all things from his sight, and he fell with the impression that he was being suddenly hurled into the night. . . .

But it was not long that he lay thus—instinct was stronger than all; besides, the warm arms of the frightened child seemed to drag him back to life, infusing new vitality into his spent frame; so he struggled to his knees, the little girl still clinging to his neck.

He looked around him, desperation in his eyes; they had reached an opening in the wood—a circular glade surrounded by gaunt trees, and nowhere a path to be seen, and nowhere the smallest sign how he could get out of this drear forest, that shut him in like forbidding walls.

He pressed the maiden's face close to his, taking comfort from the soft cheek that was laid against his.

And the child stood beside the kneeling man, and gently with timid hands stroked his tumbled locks, all the time peering at him with anxious attention.

Eric was still too weak to rise to his feet, so he remained

kneeling, scanning the solitudes with hopeless bewilderment. The wind still howled through the tree-tops, from which dismal voices seemed to be chanting ever the same dreary ditty, and sometimes it rose to such a din that it was more like unto the wild songs of savage hordes carrying their dead to the grave.

The falcon was nowhere to be seen ; even that companion had flown away, so that they were alone—quite alone—in this fantastic, oppressive wilderness.

A last shine of daylight still rested over all, and with horror clutching at his heart Gundian now perceived that running in lines all over the snow that lay before him were small footprints resembling those of a dog ! Ah ! but no dogs could inhabit so forsaken a forest ; the kindly friend of man would not lose his way amongst these impenetrable thickets ; those marks in the snow had quite another explanation, confirming the fear he had had before ;—but something must be done : action would revive him,—he could not remain thus to perish miserably without trying at least to save the treasured child.

With a superhuman effort he rose to his feet,—for a moment his young body swayed like a sapling in the wind ; but he would not—would not give way ! What was to be done ? He had heard that great fires frightened off beasts of prey—a small flame even was supposed to keep them at bay ; and he remembered the legend of a maiden wandering alone in a forest with only a small lamp in her hand protecting her from harm,—surely he would not be weaker than she. Bending down to his companion he told her to help him to gather dry twigs in the underwood ; he blew upon her frozen fingers which were stiff and icy like his own.

From his pocket he took the precious box, and together they shared one of the remaining tablets which revived them in an extraordinary way; a smile even came back to the face of the wee innocent at his side.

Now with feverish haste they were gathering fallen branches from under the hostile trees, that angrily bent their mighty heads towards them, but were unable to reach down to anything so far beneath.

The bundle grew and grew, and in their absorbing work they for a moment forgot the terrors around; once even the small girl's voice rang out in a merry laugh, as she dragged a heavy log behind her, almost as large as herself. Soon Eric was crouching beside the stack they had collected and trying with his icy fingers to make the sparks fly from his flint;— many a time did he hit the hard stone in vain, but at last a welcome sound was heard—a soft crackling that became louder, till at last a bright flame shot out over the dry timber they had so patiently heaped up. Both frozen wayfarers stretched out their numbed hands to the saving warmth. As they did so they smiled at each other from either side of the burning faggots; the cheering glow lit up their pinched and tired faces, giving them again the radiant look of health.

"Come to me, little one," cried the man, and the small creature flew into his arms; then settling himself down, his back against a tree, quite near the blazing fire, he folded the forlorn little being tightly within his arms, his cloak drawn close over her, regardless of his own comfort, only thinking how to protect her against the deadly frost of the night.

He took his sword from its sheath and laid it down beside him within reach of his hand.

Long he sat thus, trying to penetrate the darkness, whilst the rhythmic breathing of his tired charge told him that for a while oblivion had mercifully descended upon her.

But it was a weary time before he dared close his own

burning eyes, so afraid was he that something dreadful might happen to the child whilst he slept.

At length Nature would have her way—his head sank on his breast, the strained arms relaxed their hold, and all the misery was wiped from his mind by the kindly wings of sleep.

XVI

ERIC awoke because the intensity of the cold was eating into his bones. The fire had died down, only a faint glow remained under the ashes; and there, oh horror! . . . seated on the other side of the small smouldering heap that once had been their protection, sat a great tawny wolf with eyes that looked straight into his, two tiny specks of phosphorescent green.

The awful beast lifted its head and gave a long-drawn, unearthly yell that echoed round the silence like the crying of a tormented soul in great agony; again and again he sent out his ghastly call, and now he was answered by other calls coming from every part of that fearful forest. The silent thickets gave forth from their secret depths stealthy pattering forms, slinking along, flashing their teeth, their tongues lolling from their dripping mouths.

A late moon had risen above the peak of the mountain, and was now throwing her pale rays over the bleached opening that spread before the young man's feet, so that he could clearly see how these wraiths assembled from all sides, called together by the baying of their leader.

So fascinated was Gundian by what he saw that for a while the immense danger he ran was almost forgotten; only the frightened cry of the child, who had awakened to see the awful creature staring at her with glistening eyes, brought him back to the reality of things.

His exhausted condition, the heavy drowsiness produced by the cold that was gradually penetrating through all his veins, had thrown a torpor over his senses, so that all appeared as in a dream.

He returned the green stare of his opponent, unable to make an effort to throw off the weakness that imprisoned his frozen limbs.

The crumbling fire was dying out more and more ; the last glowing twigs fell together with a faint fizzing sound, that made the leading monster rise in fear and move back a few steps, still kept in awe by the narrow frontier of heat that alone separated him from his victims.

For one more deadly moment there was a pulsing silence and then . . . the beast sprang with a great leap on the seated man.

In a moment Eric was on his feet, sword in hand, throwing himself before the terrified child, that at all costs he meant to protect ! And with a furious blow, although he had been quite unprepared for so sudden an attack, he split the skull of his raging enemy.

Eric had never used arms before ; war had not been his vocation ; he loved peace and pleasure and all things that make life beautiful and sweet.

But now he stood up like a tried warrior, his blade flashing under the rays of the moon ; alone he advanced against the ferocious beasts that all rushed in upon him with sudden rage to avenge their fallen chief.

He knew not from whence he took his strength ; but he stood before them like a figure cast in bronze, defending himself, keeping them at bay with the point of his precious sword. But for each savage animal that fell beneath his frantic defence another seemed to spring up in its place—always more and more, till their baying filled the silent night with hideous clamour.

Hell seemed to have opened its doors. All round Eric and the child, who was crouching in an agony of fear close behind him, were blazing eyes, sharpened fangs, ravenous bleeding jaws, a medley of dark fighting bodies falling over each other with angry yells, as they one and all rallied against the single youthful hero, who stood facing them, the blood streaming from the blade of his sword.

Blood fell also in great dark drops from his lacerated hands, where more than one murderous tooth had left its mark. His pale brow was streaked with red; from off his shoulder his coat had been partially wrenched, and a great gash gaped through the torn tissue.

Still he stood his ground; many a rugged body lay dead at his feet, but always more roaring foes seemed to descend upon him, a whole army of hungry, voracious fiends that had sworn his destruction.

His force was giving out, he clearly felt that the unequal battle could last no longer; only a miracle could now save them both.

His arm became inert; the blood flowed from the open wound in his head in a trickling stream down into his eyes, clouding his sight, so that he could no longer direct his strokes.

Yes, all was over now; he was not to be of those who win. . . . This was to be the end . . . the end. . . . But what was this? From beneath his clenched fingers a dazzling glare had suddenly broken forth — a glare so intense and blinding that for a moment he could see nothing but its luminous rays! Had really a miracle come to pass? Was he dreaming? But no . . . his awful assailants were rapidly retreating with furious groans, as if unable to bear the sight of the thing he held in his hand!

What was it that suddenly cowed their savage force? Then all at once he understood. . . . The crystal hilt of his sword was blazing with light!

He fell on his knees, his forehead pressed against the shining cross, his eyes closed, his head bent in awful fatigue. But peace had come over him—a great and wonderful peace. The beasts of prey were backing, always farther, from this awesome light that had so miraculously fallen upon them.

With hanging heads they retreated, their piercing eyes fixed upon the fiery symbol they dared not face. They backed and backed, till they were but a mass of darkness, out of which their eyes glowed like a circle of Easter tapers held by pious hands in adoration before that cross of flame. Alone in the middle of that moonlit glade knelt Eric, quite still, as in a trance; the point of his sword had reddened the snow on the ground; the hilt seemed fashioned out of the stars of heaven.

The moon looked down upon his golden locks, transforming them into a mass of silver; even his torn and travel-stained clothes were turned into glowing metal like a knight of olden days.

From the shadow of the giant trees the little girl came slowly forward, and on reaching the spot where Eric prayed with lowered brow, she, too, fell on her knees and advancing her innocent lips kissed the blade of the sword.

XVII

Now also the forest had been left behind. Upon the snowy covering of the silent glade many a gaunt body lay still and cold, nor will we ask in what manner their hungry companions visited them when the flashing cross was to be seen no more.

Eric was now fighting his way to reach the highest peak that shone far above the clouds. Never would he be able to relate how he had found his way out of that forest where at first all had seemed united against him to hinder his progress.

The morning after that night of battle which had so gloriously ended, Eric had walked as in a dream, the cross-shaped hilt held against his breast like some crusader in a distant land. Alongside of him trotted the little girl clinging to a corner of his cloak. He knew not why, but everything around him had lost the hostility of the night before ; his feet moved easily over the frozen snow without sinking beneath the surface.

The giant trees were a wonder of brilliant white ; during the early hours of morn a vapoury mist had fallen over the sleeping immensity, and the coming day had transformed all around into a fairy wood of dazzling gems.

Each separate branch stood out in crystallized splendour, each needle, each hanging cone had become a transparent jewel, radiating all the colours of the rainbow.

The tiniest plant that had pushed its way through the snow, the driest, humblest twig, the most common stone, all had been conjured into a miraculous treasure of light which the most cunning human art could never have fashioned. It was a joy beyond words to the eye, a splendour God's nature alone could produce.

All was now peace and stillness; through the mighty rows of glittering tree-tops the sun shot slanting rays that lit up the snow like a field of golden flowers; and beyond, distant glimpses of the sky were visible, pink like roses of the East gathered together by some enamoured king to be strewn under the feet of his beloved.

The sombre pines had other faces beneath their fairy coating of frost, and seemed now to greet him like some honoured guest, bending their crowns in sign of homage.

On he walked without any feeling of fatigue, never once stumbling on his way.

The falcon was again flying before him like a white kerchief waved in token of greeting; . . . the higher they climbed the rarer became the trees and the wider did the blushing sky spread before their eyes.

Now they were out in the open once more, climbing from rock to rock; and when Eric turned round to look down upon the forest that lay far beneath, like a magician's garden of gigantic frosted flowers, he perceived that the ghostly army of lost souls was once more following close in his rear. Where had they been during that night of terror? Had they lain in waiting till he had fought himself through that dangerous trial? Had they trembled and feared that he was to be overthrown and their forlorn hope destroyed?

There was a great and frowning height still before him which he had to scale; but on this early morn so charged with brightness, his heart was full of faith, and again there was a song on his lips; but now it was one that had a deeper meaning. So with a shout of anticipation he lifted his hand and waved it to the silent followers; then, pointing to the rocky peak that appeared above the snow and clouds like a sunlit dream, he rushed forward with unfaltering step, as if he had only just started upon his ascent. The little girl was always near him; she, too, was full of the joy of the morning. . . .

But night came on, and still they were toiling. The shining peak had veiled itself with a cloud of darkness; the bitter cold of the mountain tops was laming their steps, so fresh and buoyant at the break of day.

Now the man had to bend down and lift the weary little soul once more in his arms.

Their friendship had turned into tender love, and as he held her in his safe embrace she covered his tired face with kisses sweet and soft like the touch of a butterfly's wing. One more awful night they spent lying fast locked in each other's arms, vainly trying to shut out the biting frost, as only protection Eric's thin black cloak.

They had mercifully discovered a cavity in one of the rocks, and there on a bed of grey moss they had slumbered fitfully, almost too exhausted to find any deep repose. And when morning came it looked down upon two haggard mortals sitting side by side, crushed one against the other, in dire distress. Their faces were pinched and livid; their teeth chattered with cold; their eyes, surrounded by deep circles of fatigue, searched about them in questioning misery. Within their numbed fingers they held an empty box! . . . But Eric's spirit was still undaunted. He meant to win! That night his dream had risen again before his eyes, more vivid and fascinating than ever.

Lately his advance had been so tedious, the efforts needed to overcome the difficulties so great, that all his faculties had been concentrated upon the single desire to save his own life and that of the child; so that the vision of the outset had been losing some of its power.

He staggered to his feet; the child hung a dead weight round his neck, she was quite unable to make further effort. What should he do? He could not leave her to perish here, this dear companion of the mountain tops!

Yet thus encumbered, how could he reach the final height? His strength was spent, his feet were bleeding, his clothes were torn, the wounds of the night before were a throbbing agony beneath the clinging arms of the little girl.

He felt that they were breaking open anew, that his warm blood was slowly trickling down on to the snow, and with each drop that fell his life seemed to be oozing slowly away. And there far above, like the tantalizing vision out of an ethereal world, rose the peak of his desire.

Again the rays of the sun reddened its crown like a glowing flower. Was it mocking him in his mortal distress? Was it luring him on to life or to death? But he must mount, always farther; he could not give up now within sight of his goal! Courage! Courage! He must conquer and win! But what were those white arms beckoning to him out of the morning mist? What were those veils of transparent vapour waving to him from the rock above? Were they apparitions out of some fantastic dream, some hallucination of his tired brain?

Anyhow he would desperately follow them, perhaps they would help him in his distress; but the higher he climbed the farther did the beckoning figures always recede; each time he had thought to reach the height where they stood he saw them far away hovering above him on some steep boulder, which again he scaled only to be baffled anew.

It was an awful pursuit, the heavy child clinging around his neck, his open wounds dripping, leaving red traces wherever he passed.

His shoes had been cut almost to shreds by the rugged rocks, so that his feet suffered an agony of pain.

A blind rage seized him against these spirits of the wilds who mocked his cruel plight; and yet, had he but known it, it was just their alluring aloofness that was helping him upon his final climb. His overwhelming longing to reach those ethereal beings with whom he hoped to find rest gave him the energy to clamber always farther, the intensity of his desire infusing almost superhuman force into his attenuated body.

Suddenly he stopped with a gasp, almost letting the child fall from his arms;—other visions were now before him floating amongst the clouds.

The indistinct apparitions had taken form, changing into white-winged angels all flying upwards, their long trailing garments mingling with the mist.

Ah! these would lead him to his last height! These celestial beings had been sent from heaven to help him in his bitterest need.

Looking down at the child in his arms, he saw that her face was deadly pale, her eyes were shut, the long lashes cast deep shadows on her sunken cheeks.

Indeed it was time to reach some shelter where he could lay her down.

Then raising his head a cry escaped his lips . . . there close before him he espied the great peak which had always appeared so absolutely beyond his reach.

There it stood, enormous and majestic, an overpowering revelation rising out of the filmy clouds—clouds that were one mass of white-robed angels, their wings bearing them upwards, their arms extended in gestures of welcome towards this pilgrim of the heights!

Eric ran forward, all his remaining energy gathered together in one last supreme effort. The blood sang in his ears, his breath came in tormented gasps, his heart beat like a giant hammer, and wherever he passed the hard stones bore marks of his dripping wounds.

With one arm he pressed his heavy burden against him, with the other he hoisted himself higher and higher, clambering with dogged persistence, ignoring both pain and danger, always onwards, his enraptured eyes fixed in an ecstasy of hope on the heavenly host that was showing him the way . . . and now . . . and now . . . he was lying face downwards on the hard snow-covered rock, his arms outstretched over the motionless body of the little girl.

He had reached the top, he had not failed ! . . . he had really won !

Long he lay in completest exhaustion unable to move, almost unable to think, or even to feel. Around him the mists rose and fell like a restless foam-covered sea !

Slowly he lifted his head, and what first met his gaze was the face of the child.

With a startled exclamation he took it in both his hands ; but it rested there limp and inert with tightly shut eyes. Convulsed with fear he bent towards it, pressing his lips upon the silent mouth, covering the waxen face with eager caresses, chafing the frozen hands, the tiny bare feet, calling to it words of love and endearment, begging it to look up and speak.

But all in vain ; no responsive smile came to the blanched lips, and when he let her slip from his arms the wee body fell back, a poor little heap, upon the ground.

Then Eric covered his face with his hands and sobbed as if his heart would break.

Thus did he remain completely overcome, in frightful distress. Oh, why — oh, why had he been unable to save her treasured life ? Why, why was he alive while she was dead ? Why had all his efforts been in vain ? Why had he reached his goal only to be crushed by this bitter grief? O God! O God! What was the use of such a thing?

But what was that? Over his head the sound of wings. . . . He let his hands fall from his tear-stained face, and looking up into the blue, blue sky above, overcome with wonder he discerned two shining angels who held within their arms the form of the poor little maid. . . .

They mounted always farther into space, and as they did so he saw the humble companion of his wanderings all bright and transfigured, like unto the angels themselves.

Before they disappeared into that vast splendour of blue, she bent toward him a face full of love and gratitude, bearing an expression of heavenly peace which descended upon his soul, revealing unto him that henceforward he need grieve for her no more.

XVIII

But the joy that is one with sorrow
Treads an immortal way
Fiona Macleod.

Eric remained for a long while, his face turned to the sky, his eyes fixed upon the spot where the bright vision had melted into the infinite.

Indeed it had been a consoling sight to see the lowly little waif changed into a shining light, her tattered rags turned into a robe as immaculate as those of the ethereal beings who had borne her away into the sky.

God had been merciful; it was better thus; all her fatigue and weariness were at an end, all the scars and wounds had been wiped from her starving body, and when she had looked down upon him it had been with a light of ineffable happiness within her eyes.

But now Eric felt how completely exhausted he was; so throwing himself upon the naked rock, he lay face downwards like one who is dead.

It was many hours before he had strength to raise his head; and when he did so, the glare of noon beat down upon him with life-giving force.

He rose to his feet looking about him, then stood in rapture before what he saw.

The peak upon which he had climbed was far above everything else, overlooking the entire universe; a frowning solitary mass. On three sides of him were mountains and steep, precipitous passes, dark and forbidding, a whole world of mystery and desolation, where human foot would not dare to penetrate ; sombre secrets seemed hidden in every crevice.

Over all brooded an implacable silence ; light and shade played on the face of the mountains in startling contrast, almost white in places, in others deep indigo ; and far away on the horizon the vast immensities dwindled into a mist of blue, like smoke rising out of some giant's caldron.

But at his feet lay what might have been a vision of the promised land, a wondrous revelation of light and beauty—as far as the eye could reach, a blooming plain all shimmering in the radiant sun, out of which a glorious expectation seemed to rise and remain suspended, awaiting some great moment of fulfilment. A heavy ripeness saturated with the glow of harvest was spread over the earth ; long roads like silver ribbons wound through this vast richness, and they were like never-ending illusions, leading always farther into a blessed region of dreams.

Broad rivers shone like molten metal as they slowly flowed between fruitful banks, in places bordered by thick forests that stood out in delicate masses against all that treasure of sunshine. A happy country indeed, if only it did not melt away when the foot reached its border.

Something near by now attracted his attention. Beneath where he stood there was a flitting to and fro, a movement in the air, something impalpable and that yet called him back to his more immediate surroundings.

Not very far below he perceived a small dark lake like an enormous eye, sombre and watchful, encased between granite boulders. Around this deep bottomless pool stood all his ghostly followers, watching with absorbed interest the water at their feet.

There was something mysterious and unusual about that green-black surface.

It was dead still; and then, quite unexpectedly, anxious convulsions would shake its depth, and out of its quiet face bubbles would suddenly rise, spreading over the whole till the entire water was covered with enormous dewdrops, and each single drop reflected within its circle the blue of the sky.

Then in places the transparent globes would detach themselves and rise into the air like giant soap-bubbles, floating away into space till they disappeared from sight; and all these bubbles were of such exquisite beauty, and so varied in hue, that Eric imagined he saw colours within them that his eye had never before looked upon.

What was the meaning of it all? What were his silent pursuers doing around that bewitched mountain lake? What were they awaiting? Why did a feeling of silent expectancy rise to where he stood?

Very carefully Eric climbed down towards that curious gathering. Noiselessly he approached, afraid of frightening them away.

As he did so, the shadowy figures one and all turned his way and fell down on their faces in postures of sudden adoration; from over their heads a whispering wind waved towards him, a wind that was full of sighs and hushed voices, like a far-off crowd always crying the same thing. Eric started back abashed, quite at a loss to know what he should do; then to his utmost astonishment he saw how the foremost spirit arose, and, giving him a last look of gratitude, without the slightest warning quietly walked into that uncanny water and disappeared beneath the surface! Following his example all the others did the same! It was but a flash!

Eric threw himself with an exclamation towards the edge, but it was too late! Every trace of them was gone, nothing remained but large circles on the face of the water. Eric looked down into the darkness, and there he saw something rising slowly to the top. . . .

It was the miraculous bubbles. One by one they appeared slowly like some fairy procession ; and when they reached the light of day they grew in size, hovered a moment over the dark element, then rose light and joyful into the sky, and as they mounted their colours changed in infinite variety, transparent globes of exquisite beauty.

Close over the water they were green and blue ; in rising their hues turned into violet and purple, that gently graduated through every tone of gold and yellow till they were one blaze of flame that quite imperceptibly faded away into the blue of the sky, where they hung suspended, hardly discernible, till at last they were one with the infinite ; and that was so high, so high overhead, that it might have been at the very gates of heaven !

Then Eric understood. . . . These were the lost souls he had freed ; all had found rest at last ; all had been able to detach themselves from this weary world always higher into the sky.

Had it really been given to him to be their salvation ? Had they found eternal peace and joy because he had not fallen on the way ? Then indeed no sacrifice had been too great, no trial, no fatigue too vast. And in sign of gratitude they had displayed before his wondering eye the most divine colours he had ever seen, filling his artist soul with the deep joy of beauty for which he never could be thankful enough.

He turned again to look at the pool, and as he did so there on the opposite bank he saw an apparition which made his heart stand still.

A very old man, tall and gaunt, wrapped in grey flowing folds, a thin cloak suspended from his shoulders, a weather-beaten hat shading his face, his long beard falling far down on his breast.

In his hands he clasped a thick stick on which he leaned. With a cry of joy Eric stretched out his hands towards that shadowy figure, for was it not his old and venerated friend the hermit!

The grey vision turned, and with hollow eyes looked at him long and earnestly, with such a wonderful expression of loving affection that it made tears gather in the boy's eyes.

But his beloved old master was also transparent and ghostly like the lost souls that had at last found peace.

Was this his spirit that had left his earthly body? Would God in His mercy grant the beautiful miracle that through his courage and persistence he should also have brought rest and redemption to this weary sinner whose precious words he could never forget?

His whole soul yearned to hear the dear tired voice once more, to drink anew from that source of wisdom which had so refreshed his spirit. Yet he had the cruel apprehension that this joy could be his no more.

"O Father, I want to hear thee speak," he cried, but no answer came from the other side of the dark water.

The old man only continued to stare.

Then an awful despair gripped at Eric's heart, for he felt as if he had lost his dearest treasure.

Why was life so cruelly full of lights and shades? Why was the full cup always dashed from the lips?

"Father, father," he cried, "I do so long for the sound of thy voice; speak, oh, speak, I beseech thee," but there was no response; only silence deep and absolute, and a second later a faint echo of his own words whispering round the granite boulders.

Then something very wonderful was revealed to his sight; there beside the old man stood a shining translucid woman, a woman whose face he could but faintly discern.

Her head was bent back and her two uplifted arms shone like rays of light, pointing to the sky.

Her long robe flowed down, a trailing mist, into the quiet water, where it hung like a cloud. And this filmy vapour wrapped itself round the feet of the man, and as it slowly mounted towards his heart a marvellous change came over the aged hermit; his astounded pupil saw how very gradually all the years rolled from him, how his bent figure became upright, and for a short moment the vision of a manly face full of strength and beauty flashed before his eyes, and then . . . everything was gone! A gust of wind swept the whole miracle into the dark lake, where a cloud of smoke alone remained.

The smoke hovered for a second, blue grey over the face of the deep; and then out of the very centre shot a quivering flame, intense and dazzling, that mounted slowly like a tongue of fire, always higher and higher, till it was lost from sight!

XIX

My eager hands press emptiness to my heart, and it bruises my breast.
　　　　　　　　　　　　　　　　　　TAGORE.

FEELING weak and completely overcome by so many conflicting emotions, Eric now began slowly to descend from the mighty height, with an intense and overpowering desire for rest and food.

He was entirely spent, knowing that he could not go much farther unless he found help in his need. This side of the mountain was much less steep than the other; it led down by soft green inclines to the happy land he saw calling to him from below.

Snow and winter, rocks and wilderness were now a thing of the past; this was quite another world, smiling and at peace.

With stumbling feet he dragged himself along.

All zest of having won was wiped out and gone. He only felt an aching longing for the little companion who had abandoned him in the hour of attainment.

Was this for ever the way of the weary earth? Were all victories so sad? He had also an unceasing desire for the voice of his old friend the hermit, knowing that he would have been able to explain what was but dark mystery to his searching mind.

He had the sensation of being completely forsaken and useless, a weary, weary stranger who had no home in this world. As he was pondering, sadly discouraged, both body and mind overwrought with fatigue, he saw the wings of the falcon waving before him, beckoning to him like some trusted friend; and this, at least, gave him a feeling of not being entirely forgotten.

So on he plodded, each limb stiff and painful, his unhealed wounds throbbing like tormented hearts, the hand at his side empty and lonely, missing the confiding touch of the childish fingers.

Heavy with misery, his head sunk on his breast, he followed the bird with faltering step, mechanically climbing always farther down, but a poor ghost of his former self, looking neither to the right nor to the left, for once quite irresponsive to all the beauty around him. He knew not how he advanced, all had become blank and colourless. As the day drew to an end he came to a wide mountain-meadow where a flock of sheep was peacefully grazing.

Before he could realize what was happening he was suddenly attacked on all sides by savage shaggy dogs that barked furiously, showing their teeth, jumping at him, and tearing at his ragged clothes.

Eric was much too tired to oppose any resistance, and no doubt it would have gone badly with him had not a shrill whistle unexpectedly made the dogs stand still, all attention, their ears pointed, listening.

A heavy stick was now flung in their midst scattering them on all sides, so that they turned and ran yelping after the peaceful sheep, masking their discomfiture by wildly scampering round the flock.

Then a quite young boy came running towards where Eric stood in dejected misery, his strength all spent, incapable of moving another step.

The shepherd youth, seeing how sorry was the plight of this stranger, went quickly up to him, and laying a strong arm round his waist asked if he could be of any help.

Eric was unable to answer; he felt the earth yielding beneath his feet; so he simply laid his head on this sturdy peasant's shoulder and let himself be led away, he knew not whither.

It was long before he came back to the knowledge of his surroundings. He must have lain in a deep swoon; but after a time he felt his head being lifted with rough kindness, whilst a bowl of warm milk was held to his parched lips. He drank in great gulps like one utterly famished; drank and drank till not a drop was left. Through his tired brain shot the thought, that hit him like an aching blow, if only his little companion were there to share this life-giving draught; then he sank back with closed eyes, still too weak to care where he was, indifferent if he was to live or die, all his nature one crying need of repose.

He slept many hours; indeed, so deep was his slumber that after a time the shepherd came to where he lay, anxiously putting his hand upon the sleeper's heart, afraid of finding it silent beneath his touch.

But he felt its regular beating against the tips of his fingers; so he left Eric where he had laid him within the humble hut and went out to his flock, leaning upon his long stick, his chin resting on his hands, looking over the mountains that were gradually fading into the shades of night. Here it was already summer, the grass grew thick and green; the cold and frost had been left up there upon the frowning heights; indeed it was a smiling contrast.

Eric slept all that night and through the following day; darkness was again spreading over the world when at last he woke.

He sat up, looking about him, trying with his numbed brain to grasp his whereabouts. The door of the hut stood wide open and close before it a big fire had been lit.

Its crackling reminded Eric, with a pang, of the great blaze that had saved him and the little maid from almost certain death. He saw again the dear soft lips smiling at him from over the jumping flames, remembered how sunken had been her eyes, and with a groan he turned his face to the wall.

But he could not keep still very long; a mighty hunger was gnawing at his vitals, he was in absolute need of finding food; so he rose stiffly from his couch, stretching his aching limbs as he went to the door to look out.

There in the flickering light of the fire sat the shepherd, a beautiful boy with large brown eyes and dark hair hanging to his shoulders, a high fur cap on his head with a flower behind his ear.

He was dressed in a white shirt and trousers, with linen bands wound round his legs; on his feet he wore sandal-like shoes kept in place by leathern thongs.

About his waist was a broad leather belt within which a flute and a dagger had been stuck, and over his back hung a coat of shaggy sheep-skin. Chin in hand the peasant sat staring with dreamy content into the flames. In a circle around him lay his dogs, their heads resting on their paws, their unkempt coats the colour of earth and autumn-leaves. Only one enormous brute was white, which kept staring at his master with watchful eyes, whilst the others slumbered and snored. It was a peaceful sight; the stars coming out one by one, and not far off the flock lay, huddled together in attitudes of repose.

Eric had moved so noiselessly that even the dogs had not heard his approach, but now as he ventured out of the hut they immediately were all upon him snarling and gnashing their teeth. The shepherd jumped to his feet and came quickly to where Eric stood with a joyful exclamation of greeting; but his guest fixed him with hollow eyes not able to utter a word.

"I know what thou needest," cried the boy, and leading Eric back into the hut he took from a chest two earthenware dishes, one of which was filled with thick creamy cheese.

"Eat," said the youth, "it will do thee good; but then I want thee to talk, for lonely forsooth are these hills; I want to hear the sound of thy voice. I live here in utmost solitude many months of the year: I guard my sheep and make this cheese. I play to the stars and sing to the sun, but they are too far above and care not to talk to me: I want to hear of thy wanderings and why thou lookest so sad. Tell me, I pray, didst thou verily come from the other side?"

Eric seized the bowl with a hasty gesture, and greedily consumed the tasty food, feeling as he ate how new strength began gradually to course through his veins. Never had he been so hungry, and this simple fare was in truth the very best dish he had ever eaten in his life!

Gratefully he looked at the young peasant, and at last he spoke:

"I cannot thank thee enough for thy spontaneous hospitality at a moment when without thy help I would surely have died of exhaustion. Thou wast sent me from God, as a sign that in His mercy He desireth me to continue my road. I have come from far, so far that to me it seems as if I had been wandering all my life."

He turned his trustful eyes to the youth, and with the smile which made him dear to every man's heart, he continued:

"Once, it may be years ago, for I have no more count of time, I lived in the palace of a king."

"Oh!" cried the boy, "why didst thou go?"

"Because," answered Eric, "I am seeking for a face which I cannot find—a face that I see in my dreams; so I had to leave all that rich ease and comfort, all that had sweetened my days, and always am I searching and still may have to wander many a mile."

The shepherd stared at him in growing astonishment, almost afraid that his strange guest might be crazy.

"It seems to me," he said, "that there are many faces on this earth; and why must thou journey so far looking for what is so easy to find? Why didst thou leave the king's palace? Forsooth, I would have remained and lived in joy and plenty"; and merrily he laughed, showing two rows of splendid white teeth.

Eric did not smile but replied:

"Ah! thou dost not understand. Dearly did I love my kingly master; and I grieve that I could not listen to his bidding. But there is something within each of us that when the time comes calls with insistent voice, and then we must leave all and follow. I am but a foolish youth, but this I have learnt: we cannot choose our lives nor in what way we desire to live them; some power there is stronger than our human will that carries us forward upon a road we do not know. I had but a short while ago a venerable master, and these were his words: 'That each man runs after the same thing, although each calls it by a different name.' The master I loved said the name he had found for it was Happiness, but that none of us realize when we have it in our hands. Why he said this I do not know. Dearly did I love to hear him talk, but not always did I grasp the meaning of his words."

"Happiness!" queried the peasant boy; "happiness! It soundeth sweet to the ear; dost thou think that thou shalt find it at the end of the way?"

Eric looked out into the flames of the fire before he slowly replied:

"The master said that we could grasp but the shadow, that the thing itself was God's. Deeply have I pondered over the sense of this saying, and this is what I have found in my mind: God hath not time for each man's clamouring, so He has strewn over the world things that shine and things that lie in the shadow; those that shine dazzle the eye and give pleasure, and those in the dark awake a longing to know, and thus God leads each man forward to search for himself, each according to his desire. But the wise man said that few reach it in the end, and when they do they seldom may keep it long. Ah! but I wish I knew! My heart is so full of longing, and yet I feel that some part of it will never be filled!"

But the peasant boy wanted to hear of other things; to him this talk was but a waste of time.

"Tell me, hast thou really climbed over this barrier of mountains; and how is it thou didst not perish on the way?"

Gundian took his sword between both hands, and looked at it with tears in his eyes:

"This sword kept me from death when I thought my last hour had come, and always, when all hope seemed at an end, something there was that saved me in my bitterest need.

"The old man of the hills believed in my power to win, and then . . ."—Eric's voice trembled as he spoke—"I had at my side a sweet little soul that providentially had been given into my care; and a curious thing have I learnt: we can do for others what we cannot do for ourselves. Many a time would I have given in and died, had not the soft hand of the child kept hold on my life by the desire I felt that it should not perish!"

And then, his hands folded over the hilt of his sword, dreamily gazing afar off, Eric related, with many words, all he had seen and done.

The eyes of the lonely rustic hung, with ever growing interest, upon the face of his wonderful companion, and many a time did a loud exclamation either of joy or fear break from his lips; and when Eric told of the vision of angels, the boy started to his feet, hands joined in an ecstasy of delight.

"Thou didst see the heavenly hosts! Oh, tell me! Tell me! Were they indeed so fair? were their wings all shining and bright? had they crowns on their heads? And were their robes of snowy white? didst thou hear the sound of their voices? did they come quite near to thee? Oh! speak, I pray!"

Eric smiled very sadly.

"They brought peace to my soul at a moment when I thought my heart would break"; and within his mind our wanderer saw the face of his little friend smiling down upon him with lips that a breath of Heaven had already kissed.

"And now," asked the youth, "where art thou going? Or wilt thou remain with me? I am very forsaken up here on this far-off meadow. But dost know, it is said that no human foot can cross those mountains that thou hast scaled; it is said that amongst those lonely heights there is eternal snow and ice, and that it is always winter there when summer smiles on us here."

"Indeed it was cold; but what has crushed my joy is that it was not given me to save the child that Fate confided to my care; and this thou must know: that at the very instant I thought I had won, the Hand of God took from me what would have made my victory sweet. Indeed I reached the highest peak, and looked down upon the whole of the world beneath . . . but . . . well, I cannot explain—because I am too unlearned.

"I fear that I may not yet understand—I know not if thus it is with all we touch; the master I loved would have told me for sure if there is a hidden explanation I cannot grasp.

"He said that all our tears and hopes were needed for the making of a single whole—maybe my despair, at that moment which was loss and victory all in one, belongs also to some link of the chain. Alas! he is gone, to come no more, and I must grope alone in the dark to find the meaning of the many questions that weigh down my heart.

"But thou must tell me now what is that sunny country I saw beneath me when I was yonder, so near the skies? It was like a land all peace and beauty, sending from below to where I stood a message of hope and promise, luring me towards its fertile plains."

"It is my country," said the peasant. "I know not if it is full of beauty and promise, but I know that I love the village in which I live, that dear to me is the small cottage where my mother sits and spins, the old well from which the girls fetch water at the hour when the sun goes down. I love the great plain where the corn waves in the heat of the summer, and the long roads that are straight and dusty, upon which the carts are always rumbling never in a hurry to reach the end.

"It is a good country; and on feast days we dance in the villages, and the girls wear skirts of many colours. But from the time when the snow has melted I come to these lonely hills with my flocks, and here I quietly remain—as sole companions my dogs, and occasionally the visit of a shepherd like myself or that of a wandering monk—till the cold blasts of autumn drive me back to the plains.

"I do not mind the solitude—I have my flute, and the dear songs of my country; and we love not overmuch to live in a hurry, or to move about with busy hands.

"My mother weaves and spins, and my sisters embroider strange designs on the shirts they will wear on the day of their marriage. Oh, indeed I love this country of mine!"

"Tell me more," begged Eric. "I love to hear thee talk. I feel then the peace of thy plains steal over my weary body that has come from so far."

"There is not much to tell," answered the boy. "Our cottages are small and are covered with shaggy roofs of thatch and maize. Large sunflowers look in at the tiny windows, and when a stranger all hot and tired comes along the road the dogs rush out from every door and the air is filled with their barking and noise.

"At the fall of night the herds come home raising clouds of dust as they pass. Each one knows the corner where it dwells, and stops of its own accord at its own gate, while the small boys run about bare-foot clacking their whips. In winter everything is deeply enveloped with snow, which lies like a cover of feathers, keeping the fields warm from the frost, and when the sun goes to bed it lights up the sky with flaming red that spreads over the snow as well ; and then black troops of crows fly across the horizon, and settle like a dark cloud upon the white immensity, flat and endless, as far as the eye can reach.

"And when spring comes the wind blows in storms and dries up the lakes made by the melting snow. Then the fields are a patchwork of black and white ; timidly the little flowers push their heads through the dead leaves in the woods, and the children run out of the villages to gather them in bunches which they sell to the passers-by. Thou must remain with me and I shall tell thee more ! "

But Eric explained that he must soon continue his road, for he knew not how far he still had to go:

"All roads will feel soft to my feet after the mountains I have climbed ; but my heart has lost its brightness and I begin to wonder what I shall reach in the end.

"At first the gladness that filled my being found an echo in each thing I met as I went along. I used to sing and play on my flute. And then came days when all was strange and full of secret dangers I could never understand.

"Later I climbed those awful mountains; much did I find there, and much did I lose. But I no more sing as once I did."

Both boys had risen and gone to the door of the hut, where they stood, hands linked, looking out on the night; and there on the stump of a tree near by sat the beautiful falcon, and round his neck the blue diamond still blazed like a consoling star. Eric went to the bird and laid his hand on its head; the faithful creature turned his way and a bright light shone in its eyes.

"This was my trusted scout, who showed me where I should go; but I fear he will no more follow me when I go down to the plains. If thou allowest I shall still spend this night under thy roof and then go my way."

"I wish I could leave my flocks," cried the youth, "and follow thee; thy face is so fair, and never have I heard voice more sweet. I fear I shall see thee no more, for thou seemest out of a world of dreams."

Eric did not reply, but stood looking into the night; then very slowly he unfastened the golden chain he still wore round his neck, and slipped it over the head of his host.

"Keep this in token that really I have been with thee; but now let me rest on thy couch, for I must leave thee soon."

He turned back into the hut, and throwing himself upon the sacks of dry leaves that formed the shepherd's bed, he was soon fast asleep, his head buried in the folds of his cloak. The sun stood already far over the mountain tops when Eric awoke after a refreshing sleep upon the primitive resting-place.

Outside the shepherd-boy was watching his sheep, leaning on his staff in his wonted attitude.

When he saw that Eric was awake he greeted him with a happy smile, and immediately set about getting him food, and a freshly milked drink, all white and warm.

Upon Eric's bidding he led his guest to a little spring near by, where at last he could wash off all traces of his past wanderings.

His wounds had been awkwardly bound up by the kind-hearted youth on the first night, while he lay in a swoon.

Eric winced with pain when the cold water came in contact with his scarcely healed skin; but it was a glorious joy to bathe in the fresh running stream, and at last our traveller felt more like his old self.

During his ablutions his host had carried off his once so neat clothes, and when he came back to the hut he found the faithful boy sewing up the rents in the rich black stuff with a long thread and needle.

He had brushed away, as well as he could, all the spots and stains, but the velvet coat and silken hose had kept little resemblance to the neat apparel in which the King's favourite had started from the white palace of the north. Eric lay down in the grass, turning his bare back to the smiling sun-rays.

Both youths joked happily together, as the peasant sewed away with diligent fingers. And when they had no more words to say, the shepherd lifted his young quavering voice and sang long-drawn ditties, which ever had a mournful ring in their notes, full of melancholy and patient longing.

Eric felt almost happy. His recent adventures seemed far-away dreams of another life; but he knew he never would be able to forget all that he had suffered, knew that the gay thoughtless boy, who had started long ago, was for ever a thing of the past.

The falcon still sat upon the stump of the tree and watched with quiet attention these two boys of such different races, the one so fair, the other so dark, both handsome and good to look upon; but no man can know what thoughts lay behind those piercing eyes.

After a while the last stitch had been put, and the kindly youth held up the velvet coat in triumph, so that the sun shone upon it making it look quite new.

"Never have I seen stuff so soft," he exclaimed, whilst he stroked the rich worn tissue with his hand.

"And it is all silk within, silvery grey, like the rays of the moon! And thou hast given me thy golden chain! Was it indeed a gift from the northern King? And to think that thou left him and all his glory to wander all over the world in search of a face! Ah! never shall I know if thou hast found it in the end! That thought is sad to me. Forsooth, I wish I could call thee brother!"

"Call me whatever thou willst," Eric replied. "I shall think of thee when I am far; for didst thou not tend me with loving care? Didst thou not feed me when I was famished and tired? Didst thou not save me when I knew I could move no farther? No brother could have done more; and one day, perhaps, we shall meet again. What is thy name?"

"I am called Radu the shepherd, and my father possesses two fields and a cart, with oxen that are grey like the stones on the road; their horns are so long that it is difficult for them to hold their heads close together; but we are poor all the same, and that is why I tend my flocks on these mountain pastures so far from my village. But if thou dost tarry for a time in yonder plains I may meet thee yet when I return to my home; but one thing I must give thee before thou goest —thy shoes are quite beyond repair—I have a couple of new sandals meant for Sunday use; they may not be what thou art accustomed to wear, but my heart will be glad if thou wilt accept so small a gift from me. Also I must see to thy wounds. I have an ointment, made by the wisest woman of our village, that can heal any sore. Come into my lowly hut and it will be my joy to dress thee and bind up thy cruel cuts!"

Eric gladly followed his kind friend, deeply touched by so much simple hospitality, and gave himself over into the clever hands of the boy: he was soon freshly bandaged with a soothing salve spread upon his aching scars.

Then he put on his neatly patched clothes, and let his host fasten the sandals on his feet, wind the long leather thongs about his legs, and tie them firmly under the knee.

Not yet content with all he had done, the boy searched about in the painted chest, and drew from its depths a long staff, richly decorated with patterns cut out of metal and fixed upon the wood with tiny nails.

"This I have worked upon for years, inventing the most intricate designs. It has been the pleasure of my lonely hours, and I want thee to have it, because never have I loved a face as much as thine; nothing so fair has ever come my way! But don't forget Radu the shepherd! It would grieve me sore!"

Now the beautiful sword was girt round our wanderer's waist, the much-used cloak hung over his back; and then, taking the boy's present in his hand, he drew the kindly friend into his arms and held him long in a warm embrace.

When the peasant lifted his head from Eric's shoulder large hot tears were running down his cheeks.

For a last time the two boys firmly clasped hands, and then Eric tore himself away. The falcon spread its white wings and flew before him leading the way.

Several times Eric turned to look his last on the comrade who had been so kind; there he stood silhouetted against the sky, leaning as ever upon his staff, his flock around him, his dogs at his feet.

XX

I saw her eyes like stars and her face pale and wonderful as dawn, and her lips like twilight water.

FIONA MACLEOD.

ERIC had now reached the base of the mountains, had actually set his foot within that fruitful, smiling plain.

One of the long roads that he had perceived from the heights lay before him.

It was covered with thick white dust, and on both sides the cornfields stood in ripening abundance, rippling in the soft wind like waves that had been dyed yellow by the rays of the sun. Bright-tinted flowers grew in the ditches—red, blue, and yellow—a feast for the traveller's eye.

Eric walked quickly; new hope had risen in his heart, his body felt rested, his spirit eager; he wondered if this would be the land of his dreams? The sun shone upon him from a cloudless sky; the crystal of his sword reflected its dazzling blue, whilst the staff he held in his hand had turned into burnished gold.

He passed many peasants as he went, and all of them turned and gazed after this stranger in silken clothes.

Eric had never lost his radiant smile; and all whom he met felt better and richer because they had looked upon the light that shone in his eyes.

Never had he seen roads so straight and so shadeless; they seemed to lead in an uncurving line from one end of the earth to the other; and those that walked upon them were never in a hurry.

Strings of carts laden with freshly cut corn and hay moved slowly along, the heads of the patient oxen bent low to the ground, straining under the weight they dragged.

High above the swinging loads long-haired youths stretched in lazy content, piped dreamy tunes upon their wooden flutes, their eyes hidden beneath broad-brimmed hats. All were dressed in the same white shirts Radu had worn.

There were also old men walking beside the vehicles, bearing heavy scythes on their shoulders.

Their faces were browned, the colour of sun-baked earth; and from under the shade of their hats silvery locks hung down covering the napes of their wrinkled necks.

One friendly peasant had bidden Eric take a rest on the top of his hay, and our wanderer had gladly accepted, swinging himself up on the swaying mass.

There he reposed among the fragrant green, half buried beneath the flowers of yesterday.

The faithful hawk flew down from the blue and perched close to his feet. Eric closed his eyes, hugging his sword to his breast; and as he did so the vision of his dream stood before him with startling vividness.

Never had he seen the face so distinctly; never had the eyes looked into his from so near. He sat up, almost expecting to find some unknown being at his side; but no—he was shut in all about by the withered grass that smelt so sweet and was so deliciously soft to his limbs.

But why had he so clearly felt his vision's sweet presence? It made his heart beat with breathless excitement. How warm the sun was! How long the road!

The clouds of dust raised by the wheels of the carts were so thick that Eric could no more see where he was going.

But had he not always allowed Fate to shape events as she would? This time again he would not worry, but simply believe in his luck as he had done all along, and trust in God who had so mercifully guided his steps.

Eric must have fallen asleep on his moving bed, because when he awoke the sun was already low and the carts had stopped beside a wood near the edge of the road. The peasants had unyoked their oxen, which were quietly chewing the cud, watching their masters with large humid eyes, their tails lazily flicking the swarms of flies from off their flanks.

The men sat in groups; some smoking, some preparing their meal of Indian corn over a small fire they had lit in the ditch.

Eric climbed down from his lofty resting-place, looking around him rather dazed from his sleep.

The falcon rose noiselessly into the air and flew off, perching upon a tall tree in the wood beyond. It had not yet forsaken its travelling companion, and Eric followed its flight with an affectionate look.

The men made room for the youth as they all sat around the boiling pot that hung over the fire from three crossed bars. One man stirred the thick dough with a solid rounded stick; from time to time they took draughts of cool water, putting their lips to the thick spouts of quaintly shaped earthen pots which were standing at their side.

None could resist our traveller's charm, and every one treated him as an honoured guest, wherever he brought his sunny smile, his dreamer's eyes, and his golden locks.

His new hosts asked him a few vague questions, about what he was doing, whither he was going, and whence he came; but they showed no great eagerness; it even appeared to Eric as if nothing could take them by surprise. In their quiet acceptation of all that came and went, they much reminded Eric of their own beasts of burden.

They did not seem to think, but only to dream, and consider one thing as good as another; they were ready to share whatever was theirs with this stranger whom they had met on the way.

In the distance a tiny village could be seen, hidden amongst thick shrubs and trees; but the peasants explained it was not their home; they still had far to go, so they meant to stop here for the night, sleeping either in the ditch among the dusty flowers or upon their loads of hay.

They kindly proposed that Eric should remain with them and rest beside their carts, which he agreed to do; but before settling down for the night he felt inclined to wander through the wood and to discover what lay beyond.

The peasants had suddenly espied the wonderful sword that hung from his belt, and they would not let him go before they had handled it in turns.

For a moment they dropped their calm in loud exclamations of approval, and stood around him as he let the blade flash in the sinking light.

Then he moved away, and soon was lost among the oaks of the wood that spread their branches over his head. Through their thick trunks the setting sun could be seen turning the sky into a burning furnace, and one side of every trunk seemed glowing hot as the fiery rays smote upon it.

A thick carpet of green spread beneath his feet, and innumerable birds sang amongst the trees as he passed. The wood was small, and before long Eric had reached the farther side.

In front of him stretched the broad bed of a river, now almost dry; but in several places the water flowed calmly along in separate streams.

The banks were bordered with grey-green willows and on the small islands in the river's bed the same trees thickly grew. The water was dyed red by the sinking sun, and each stone shone like a jewel, as if some wasteful king had cast all his treasure away.

There, where the river was dry, Eric perceived a group of small brown tents, like giant withered leaves, that the parting sun was turning into every shade of rust and orange.

Little columns of smoke mounted into the air on all sides, throwing their blue veil of filmy vapour over the bushes in the background.

Tied up to some trees near by were lean, hungry-looking horses of all sorts, and solemn grey donkeys wandered about amongst the loose stones cropping each blade of grass they could find.

Eric descended the small bank that separated the wood from the river and hesitatingly approached the shabby tents. As he did so a whole swarm of nut-brown children came running towards him, from every corner, with outstretched, begging hands, their rags hanging in tatters around their thin little bodies.

Some were quite naked and as dark as mahogany, with enormous black eyes and feathery lashes. They screamed and chattered, and many of them turned mad somersaults over the stony ground to attract the wanderer's attention.

In a second the whole settlement was in a violent uproar of excitement, mixed with the barking of dogs.

From each dwelling dark, curiously clad men and women trooped out.

Many were beautiful, and all had marvellous eyes; the younger men wore their hair in thick black curls, hanging about their faces. There were frightful old hags amongst them draped in discoloured garments that almost fell from their withered limbs, held only together by broad scarlet girdles that were wound innumerable times around their waists.

One or two young girls were startlingly handsome; they

stood with heads thrown back, their hands on their hips, holding short white pipes between their flashing teeth.

Their tresses were bound in gaudy rags, and each wore a flower of brightest hue stuck behind her ear. Round their necks they had hung strings of beads and shells, of all sorts and sizes, that shone in varying colours as they moved about.

They were slim and upright, with narrow hips and beautiful feet and hands, but one and all were as dark as Indians, their faces having taken the tint of the long roads they were for ever pursuing.

As Eric had immediately guessed, this was a troop of that mysterious race of gypsies that comes from no one knows whither, and wanders over the world with no destination in view. Everywhere they are dreaded by the quiet inhabitants of the villages, for they are ready to steal all that comes their way, and never respect what belongs to another.

At the slightest provocation their knives are ready to spring from their belts; their tempers blaze like scorching flames; to them it seems but part of the day's work to leave a dagger within the heart of any who have awakened their resentment.

Now they all clamoured and yelled as they dragged at his cloak, touched his clothes, fingered his sword, and nearly pulled the staff from his hand.

But they were all laughing and excited, evidently enchanted to meet so fair a traveller who had so unexpectedly fallen in their midst.

Eric felt quite confused by this turbulent greeting, and was wondering what was going to happen next, when one of the quite old women moved out of the mob, took hold of his cloak, and pulled him towards her tent.

She was clothed in an old carpet-like cloth that she had wrapped round her loins over a discoloured shift that might once have been white, but was now the shade of the earth;

the whole was held together by a long band of faded colours that was twisted several times round hips and waist. Her grey hair hung in thin strands over her face, that was wrinkled and brown like the bark of a tree, but which still showed signs of former beauty. She was bent almost double, and dragged herself along with the help of a twisted staff. Like all the others she had a short white pipe in her mouth, and her head was covered with a kerchief of brilliant colour.

From her belt hung a curiously shaped shell, a sign that she was a teller of fortunes, and therefore a respected personage amongst this troop of nomads.

Eric followed her without resistance, but hesitated at the entry to her dark dwelling, very reluctant to penetrate within anything so unclean ; but the old woman was insistent, and our young traveller had to yield and even to take his place upon some indescribable rags that served as a bed and seat all in one.

The air was stifling and full of smoke, the whole place so devoid of cleanliness that Eric hardly dared to look about. The gypsy took his hand in hers, but Eric found great difficulty in understanding what she was saying, in spite of the knowledge that had come to him through the old man's tablets. With her bony finger she began following the lines on his palm. Outside the tent the other gypsies stood jabbering and laughing.

All of a sudden the old woman gave a start, and declared that whatever his fate had been, now he was near a critical moment in his life, and must expect either a great joy or a great pain, she could not tell which ; . . . "but," added the old creature, " great joy and great pain lie very near together, and often one rises out of the other ; it is hard to say which is nearer truth.

" I am the wise woman of this wandering people ; from near and far they come to listen to my words ; much could I tell thee of what I have seen, for there is not a road on this earth upon which my weary feet have not moved.

"If thou wilt not hurry away I shall tell thee many a tale; but to-day I can show thee something which we call the treasure of our clan, though in truth it belongs not to us; we believe, however, that it brings luck to our wandering tribe. Come quickly, before the light bids us farewell."

The strange old thing again seized our astonished traveller and dragged him after her out of the tent.

The rest of the dark mob wanted to follow, but the fortune-teller, who seemed to be the respected head of this curious people, stopped them with loud imprecations, and none dared oppose her wishes. She told them to go back to their camp, because she alone had the right to lead the fair stranger whither she would—that he was her guest and she would have none of their noisy company.

With incredible agility for her age she led the way, over several streams of shallow water, over rolling stones and wet sand, to a small island in the middle of the river's bed. Eric marvelled at the rapidity with which she moved along, helping herself with her stick; above their heads the white falcon flew, as always, showing the way.

Here the willows grew thick and grey, trailing their sinuous branches down to the ground where they mixed with earth and sand.

The gypsy parted the thick boughs, and as she did so a sound of sweet music came wafted on the air, dream-like, something within its notes that was at once both ghostly and unreal, something that made the heart stand still in an ecstasy of wonder.

Eric's leader scrambled up the steep bank, still firmly clutching his cloak, and almost ran along, winding her way in and out, amongst the thick growth of shrubs.

There was deep shade here in this silent place. A soft grey-green light was over all, only from between the leaves the sky could be seen blood-red.

The ground was covered with a thick carpet of harebells the colour of an Italian sky ; they swayed their heads with a tinkling sound whenever a breath of wind stirred the air.

It was a spot where fairies would surely dwell, mysterious, cool, and full of secret promise.

And there, in the midst of this carpet of blue, leaning against a moss-grown crumbling tree, was a spirit-like being out of another world !

No words can describe what Eric felt !

He only knew he was at the end of his way . . . that all his wanderings were not in vain—that something marvellous and unspeakably sweet had suddenly flooded earth and sky, that the entire universe had become one song of praise, one cry of hope, one yearning desire of fulfilment. . . .

There, before him in all their wonder and perfection, were the face and eyes that had stolen the peace from his soul and the art from his hands.

He fell on his knees, overcome by the surging emotion that filled heart and brain.

He could not grasp this amazing miracle that completely overwhelmed his being ; the hermit's words alone rang in his ears : " It may not come in splendid raiment with a crown on its head, but keep thy heart open as well as thy eyes. . . ." Yes, his eyes and heart both were open and a glorious light swept over his life, like a warm wave before which all resistance gives way, covering both past and future, with an immense longing for perfect achievement.

And this was the vision that had been at last revealed to the eyes that had searched with such tireless persistence, with such strong and faithful belief in the ultimate crowning of their desire : A girl, slim and ethereal, clad in the garment of poverty, a shirt-like dress over which a colourless scarf had been many times wound till the delicate figure resembled that of an Egyptian fresco; feet and arms were bare, and of utmost perfection.

From under a wreath of fragile harebells streamed the most exquisite tresses ever seen—rich brown in tone, but the sun had shone on them so lovingly long, that a haze of golden red had been breathed over them by all the rays that had ceaselessly caressed their softness.

She stood, her head thrown back; within her hand she held an old violin on which she was playing like one in a far-off world, for whom neither turmoil nor strife can exist, playing like an angel from the regions above, where no sin and no sorrow can have place. . . .

But her face. Oh! her face . . . in truth it was not of this world!

A radiance seemed to illuminate it from within, a shine that could come but from a soul in touch with the infinite, a soul full of light and love and hope, that no material distance could sever from its perfect communion with God. And then her eyes! Large and grey, with a far-away look—eyes that see visions and dreams past the knowledge of man; starry and clear, yet deep as a summer sea; eyes in which lay hidden all the boundless illusions of our human race, mixed with a peace that has no name.

Above her head the leaves rustled with a whispering sound; the flowers trembled, shaking their bells in waves of blue. The last glow in the sky fell slanting through the branches upon the girlish figure, till she appeared to be a transparent apparition out of the legends of yore.

Serenely indifferent to the two who watched her in rapture and silence, she played her heavenly music, a distant hymn to a being she alone could see; and upon invisible wings the gentle evening breeze carried the rippling notes far away into the fading red of the sky. . . .

The old woman came quite near to Eric and whispered in his ear :

" They say that she is mad ; but I know things that lie deeper than the deepest ocean, which they never can understand ; however, I shall teach thee some of my wisdom : God has pressed His lips on her eyes, so she ever sees visions we earthly mortals have not the power to conceive.

" She is not one of us ! She is of a race as far removed from ours as the sky is removed from the earth. But those that live in the dust, whose feet move amidst the mud of the roads, cannot believe that a creature so spotless and pure can exist in this world and yet never soil its perfection !

" So they say she is daft and turn lightly away from a problem too deep for the comfort of their shallow souls : for verily it is easier to disbelieve what the common brain cannot fathom."

" But who is she ? " queried Eric, with bated breath.

" Ah ! that we shall never know.

" In a distant land far over the sea we were once wandering on a rich-coloured autumn morning, and there we found, on the grey steps of a church, an infant of marvellous beauty. Her pearly limbs were enfolded in fine linen and lace. We had mercy upon the innocent babe, for our hearts have not the colour of our faces ; and since that blessed day she has been the joy of our tribe and the pride of both young and old.

" But when she grew to the age when she could talk, not a syllable could we understand. Her eyes for ever were searching the skies, and her words spoke of things she alone could perceive. Even I, who am wise, could not follow her sayings.

" But gradually an inner voice told me that there was something holy about this stranger maiden, something which removed her far from us, something that mortal hands should not touch.

" Then I understood that God had laid His hand upon her

brain. Now she seldom speaks, but always plays these heart-rending notes. Hark, fair stranger, listen if it is not unearthly and sweet."

Eric listened with all his soul; never before had such music come to his ears.

It was full of tears, and sighs, and hopes, and dreams; it was heavenly indeed, and yet a sobbing human chord pierced the whole, with a never-ending cry for the things that every poor mortal needs. It rose and fell, carried upon the changing tides of love and hope; it contained a yearning effort, a boundless longing, towards that land of chimeras and dreams beyond the boundaries of the earth.

Every chord seemed strung to a pulsing heart bound and fettered, yet gasping to be free.

Then it changed into an intensity of peace, like the soft winds of night descending slowly upon the heat and toil of the day; dying away into fading notes always fainter and sweeter, like the first breath of spring over sleeping woods, like the hushed voice of a great sadness that can still hope and believe . . . and then, quite suddenly, there was silence, and only the summer breeze stirred amongst the boughs of the trees.

XXI

> At last !
> The fount of beauty, Fountain of all dreams,
> Now am I come upon my long desire.
>
> FIONA MACLEOD.

EACH day Eric came to this spot of beauty to look upon the being who was the realization of his soul's desire.

But the terrible mystery, that God allowed, was that this girl never even seemed to see that he was there.

Eric Gundian, who was adored of all—Eric of the golden locks, Eric the sweet-voiced,—could not make her eyes realize his presence.

The wandering people had received him into their hearts, as every man did upon whom he turned and smiled. They gave him a tent and begged him never more to depart.

But the living dream he had come so far to seek remained in a world of her own, to which he could not find the key. The dark tribe felt no rivalry towards this being of light who had so suddenly appeared in their midst. They saw that he was a creature apart, made of another clay, filled with another life ; something that they could dearly love, but never completely understand.

Like the rough seamen on the ship, they hoped he would for ever cast in his lot with theirs and not depart as suddenly as he had come.

Zorka, the old fortune-teller, was his daily guide ; and they all considered it natural that this glorious youth should have fallen beneath the spell of the mad girl, who was their greatest pride and deepest grief.

Had they not sought in turn a smile from her lips, a look out of the wonder of her eyes, and had she not always seen past them, far beyond, into horizons all her own, never noticing the glowing worship that was cast at her feet?

Now they watched with growing anxiety if this handsome stranger would move her heart and bring her eyes down to this earth. They both hoped and feared.

They longed that the miracle should come to pass, and yet, in the deepest recesses of their hearts, there was not one who did not jealously dread the moment when, perchance, she might turn in love to this youth they knew was not as they. But none feared so much as old Zorka the witch—because had she not read within the flames of the fire, within the flight of the birds, within the forms of the smoke, within the ripples of the wave-kissed sands, that this maiden was not for earthly love, that the day when mortal lips should touch her with human caress she would fade away like vapour on the sea!

Indeed she may have erred in the reading of the signs, but it would be for the very first time in her life. So she cursed the day when she had led this beautiful boy into the presence of the girl she adored. And yet—and yet—can ever Fate be turned from the path upon which she glides? Must not one and all drink from the cup which has been fashioned for each separate lip?

Stella she had called the stranger maiden—Stella, because of her shining orbs; and no doubt when God needed her amongst His other stars, He would then take her for His very own. Ah, the wise woman, with her weak and trembling hands, how could she change the course of the moving worlds!

So she sat by her fire and stared into the bluey flames, her old head bent, her knotted palms resting on her knees, puffing away at her pipe of clay, seeing weird shapes in the smoke that rose quivering to the sky.

So much had she seen, so much . . . so much:

Lands of sunshine and regions of snow, storm-tossed waves and calmest sea, visions of beauty and visions of pain ; men that live in the clear light of day and men that crawl in the shadows of night. She had seen things that had their beginnings in joy, and things that ended in sorrow, creatures that live and creatures that die, women that love and others that hate. Murder she had seen ; and her ears had heard the last groaning sighs of the dying, as they had hearkened for the sounds of hope when the human soul was being cast naked into this world of sorrow.

The beginnings and the ends. Yes, everything had come her way,—her eyes were dim and tired from having seen all too much !

And now as she waited here not far from that island of promise, she knew that the youthful wanderer was giving all his soul in an agony of hope and expectation. She knew she was poor and helpless before these mysteries of life ; that at times even the wisest hands must hang in idle rest.

Yes, day by day Eric came and sat beside this treasure he had found, and yet it was still as far removed as in the days when he was only dreaming.

Instead of in sleep, now his waking sight drank in the vision which was part of his living being. But although he had poured out every supplication and ardent prayer his mind could conceive, he never could imprison a single look that he knew was conscious of his presence.

She sometimes would talk, but more often she would play upon her beloved violin, and then Eric would feel that each drop of his blood was rushing through his veins like a mountain torrent; or he would be possessed by a frantic longing to be free of his body to soar with the music far up into heaven.

It would happen that she would take hold of his hand and lead him to places of strangest solitude, and there her visionary words would try to describe the marvellous things her brain was seeing.

He followed the flight of her extraordinary thoughts; but each day he was filled with deeper depression, knowing that never had she consciously looked at his face, never had she realized that it was an unusual companion who was now at her side, that she was alone with a being consumed by love.

She talked in a confiding voice as a child speaks to its mother, or as one that had the habit of conversing alone in the night.

The things she said, and conjured up before his eager mind, were saturated with such unheard-of sweetness that Eric lived in a world he had never known.

And so the days passed one by one; the bluebells faded and died, and still Eric clung to the forlorn hope that Stella's eyes would suddenly open and see him at her side. The gypsies folded their tents and moved farther on, roaming from spot to spot.

Wherever they went Eric was always with them.

For hours he would walk in the dust of the roads, keeping pace with the bare feet of the woman he loved.

The falcon was always there, and still flew like a white banner before him, as it had done on the very first day. But now Eric no more followed the shine on its wings; he was following a lowly maiden who held his beating heart within her careless hand.

He passed through many villages such as Radu had described: the savage dogs rushed out and surrounded their wandering procession, the maize-thatched cottages had their doors wide open, and it was true that the tall sunflowers could peep in at the tiny windows, and that the maidens sat upon the thresholds drawing their tireless needles through the snowy linen that lay in their laps.

The peasants looked at the earth-coloured travellers with glances of disdain; and seldom did a kindly welcome greet them as they came.

Only for Eric they made an exception, and more than one dark-eyed girl would have given much to keep him at her side.

Autumn was turning the leaves into glorious colours. The woods were a never-ending marvel of red, gold, and brown. On the freshly reaped maize-fields the Indian corn lay in small pyramids of ripest orange. The peasants sat about in groups singing the songs of harvest, whilst the early night did its best to hurry the glowing sunsets out of the flaming sky.

Always smaller grew the hope in our wanderer's heart, always more weary were the endless roads.

Stella still had her eyes turned upon things he could not see. He had not been able to make her grasp the fact that she had a stranger at her side.

Each day he brought her another wreath for her burnished tresses—a wreath that he wound with his artist fingers from whatever flowers he could find along his road.

They were becoming scarcer and rarer because of the descending autumn that lay like a hush over the tired world. He made them of pale-tinted crocuses that hung upon her forehead like tired sighs—he bound them with the brightest leaves of the season that resembled the spreading sunsets he so loved at the end of the day. Often he had plucked shining berries that surrounded her waxen brow like heavy drops of blood. And one day the wreath he brought her was all feathery and white, plaited with the fluffy ghosts of the wild clematis that climbs over rock and tree.

On a morning when the clouds hung heavy over their heads he pressed above her lovely face a garland of sloe-berries entwined with grey leaves of the weeping-willow; they fell about her delicate temples, touching her rounded cheeks with loving caresses as a mother's hand would do.

Once as she sat on a hard heap of stones, spent after the tramp of the day, he left her to glean from the barren fields ripe ears of corn that had been scattered by the reapers on their way.

He made them into a golden crown which he laid at her feet in the dust, looking into her eyes, trembling under the weight of his love.

And always he found some lowly plant which he plucked with the thought of bringing a smile to her lips. He even conjured into a circlet of silver the star-shaped thistles that grew amongst the wilting grass, and so that their prickles should not wound her delicate skin, he lined it with soft green moss that lay close against her forehead, guarding it from the slightest scratch.

But the days when he found neither flower nor plant he felt like a beggar that dare not come before the face of his queen. . . .

Often when the roving tribe had pitched their tents for the night, Gundian would go and sit beside the fire with old Zorka the witch, and he never wearied of the tales she told, listening, with interest that was always new, to the quaint words that fell from her lips.

Zorka's heart had made him her own, and she dearly loved to have him at her side; but never did she find the needed courage to urge him to relinquish his quest; yet, as the days rolled by, she feared more and more that the signs might really come true.

On a night when all was dark and still, the very old woman

and the beautiful youth sat side by side looking into the leaping flames.

Zorka raised her careworn face and scanned his thinning cheeks, his sunken eyes, and the beautiful hands that were nervously clasped on his knee. Her old heart ached with fearful desire for all that could not be.

" Son, my son ! " she suddenly cried, " ah that I could tear the stars from the sky and throw them before thy feet ! Oh that I could drag down the rays of the moon and hide them all in thy breaking heart to stop thy longing ! that I could draw out all the richness of the earth and give it to thee, so that thou shouldst be at peace ! But thus it is the wide world over ; we think we have reached our soul's desire, and then we stand before it empty of all our hope."

As she spoke, sweet sounds of music came floating out of the dark—the soft notes of a violin in which all the sorrow of the earth seemed concentrated beneath the rippling cadence of joy.

Eric covered his face with his hands, and Zorka felt the burning tears rise to her dim old eyes, but she brushed them hastily away with the back of her hand.

" Dear young one," she said, " what can I do for thee ? Hast thou not told me that thou wast once a great artist with fairy fingers, and that thou didst come all this endless way through joy, sorrow, and danger, in search of a face . . . and now. . . . Oh, I have guessed it since many a day thou hast found that face—but where is thy art ?

" Crave not for what thou canst not have, but cling to that which God has given thee. If I get thee brush and colour wilt thou try and create that face for a second time ? Create it so that all should wonder how human hands could ever have been able to paint so glorious a treasure. When we cannot have the thing itself we must try and grasp its shadow."

"Oh!" cried Eric, "my old master said that the thing is God's."

"I do not know," said old Zorka, "if we pray to the same God, thou and I. Human beings always need forms into which they press their worship, but I, who am old, can tell thee this : there is but one God for all, and each man shapes Him according to the depth and breadth of his own little soul.

"When we are children and play on the ground we are taught to call Him Father ! When we grow up we long for Him as a friend, but if He keeps His smile for others we curse Him and turn our backs and say we do not believe He exists. But when grief and despair knock at our door, we long to feel Him near us once more, but we have lost our way. We grope in the dark, we hit our hands and our heads, we cry, and we moan, we stumble and fall till we are laid low in the dust.

"Then it is long till again we look up. Our hair is bleached, our backs are bent, our eyes are dim, and faltering our step ; but gradually we see all things as they were meant to be—we have left hope far behind, all that shone and was sweet knows us no more ; our way is without either light or shade, it is grey and smooth like the ocean after the storm has gone by.

"We believe that its colour will never be anything but grey ; but one day a faint light spreads very far over the most distant horizon and our tired brain begins to perceive that that light is coming slowly towards us, slowly—slowly—till it reaches our heart . . . and that light means peace that passeth all human understanding ; peace, the ultimate promise of that God we had cast away ; peace, the blessing of our snow-white hair, the last hope of our ended pilgrimage. But, my boy, wilt thou do as I bid, and create with thy hands the face thou lovest so well ? "

"I cannot, I cannot," sobbed Eric, his face all convulsed

with pain; "I have lost my art and lost my belief. I am now only one consuming passionate desire."

"Dear one that I love," answered sadly the old nomad, "for what hast thou climbed so high if thou now wilt not look up? I tell thee that if thou wilt grasp the talent that belongs to thee thou shalt find a relief beyond all thou darest to hope.

"I have been reading the signs out of the wind-swept clouds, and I know that thus help will come to thee."

"Ah, but, Mother Zorka, tell me, will she ever look at me with eyes that see?"

"Her eyes do see, my son, and although thy face be the fairest my old brain has ever conceived, canst thou know if the vision her mind is for ever adoring is not of a beauty far beyond our dreams?

"Certain flowers are not there to be plucked.

"Why the great Being of the skies has brought thee through pain and danger, drawn thee into this distant land, to dash the full cup from thy thirsty lips, after having smilingly led thee so far—is a mystery I cannot explain.

"But dost realize what it would be if thou shouldst pluck the flower too soon and thy touch be too rough, and the petals fall fading to the ground; dost know how empty then thy hands would be?

"Do as I tell thee, make that heavenly face thy very own by drawing it with the artist hands thy God has given thee! I love thee well, but I have loved her longer than thee. If the day is to come when her heart shall open to earthly passion, her eyes to the dear sight of thy face, let that day be blessed and hold it fast if thou canst.

"I shall only look on; for that is the weary lot of those who live in the past: but once more I tell thee, paint, oh, paint her face—the time may come when it will be too late!

"But now go to thy tent, for I am tired and the night is cold."

Eric rose sadly and threaded his way through the sleeping camp, past the fires that were burning low, past the patient groups of tired horses, till he reached his bed.

But Zorka sat still many an hour, following the shadowy road of her past, her dim eyes fixed upon the glowing ashes, speaking to the Being who rules our destinies, and asking over again the eternal, unanswered " Why ? " looking up to the too distant sky which for ever keeps its mystery to itself.

XXII

> He seeks to know
> The joy that is more great than joy
> The beauty of the old green earth can give.
>
> FIONA MACLEOD.

ZORKA kept her promise; and one day, who knows whence, Eric found all he needed for beginning the picture the old woman had commanded him to paint.

The tents had been pitched quite near to a forest all shining and shimmering in every shade of gold; gold under foot, gold overhead, gold falling softly from every bough.

The sun threw his glinting rays upon all the beauty that was a last glorious farewell Nature was taking from the departing year. The smoke of the camps and the mist of the autumn mornings mingled like spirit souls, and waved in moving vapours, veils that some fairy might have hung over the branches to fill her dwelling with mystic shadows and shades. From within the shelter of the wood, the great naked plain could be seen as far as the eye could reach, but the waving ocean of corn was a past dream of the summer months.

Now the fields and pastures looked desolate and barren, dark and cold, even beneath the face of the kindly life-giving planet that shone down upon it with a friendly face.

The rusty tents resembled dwarf pyramids standing upon some desert seen from afar off.

But the forest was a palace fit for a king, fashioned out of lustrous rays all woven together into a web of sunny yellows, and there sat Eric for many an hour trying to make his picture live.

Stella never refused to let him take her hand, and followed him meekly whither he led. He seated her upon a bank of grass, having first covered it over and over with leaves of fiery red.

For her lovely feet he made a nest of warm green moss, and at her side he laid a sycamore leaf full of jet-black brambleberries as polished as agate balls.

Out of their flexible branches he wound a wreath about her head; their fading leaves made a many-tinted crown, more beautiful than a queen could wear, all amber, topaz, and burnished gold, deep and rich in hue, splashed in places as with stains of blood.

In and out among the rusty leaves he had plaited dark purple aster stars that nestled among her waving hair. Whilst his nervous fingers were by slow degrees laying hold of his forsaken art, Stella played him ancient tunes of such melting sweetness that often his hot tears flowed down and mixed in crystal rivulets with the colours on his palette. As she played, all the visions of the days of his wanderings rose up out of the distance and floated like shadows before his brain.

He saw little Oona playing with her balls on the smooth marble terrace, saw the sleepy little town with the scarlet bunches of geraniums, heard the bird-like voice of the unknown girl singing her song of innocence. He walked again under the face of the moon into the ice maiden's snowy castle, and there he stood with her amongst the beating, broken hearts that lay awaiting the great trumpet call. He stood on the wave-tossed boards of the frail little vessel, mingling his voice with the cries of the sea.

Then, wandering through the enchanted grottos, he came to the place where he shudderingly knelt by the murdered form of the far too entrancing woman. In the ruined cathedral the Virgin's eyes once again blessed his folded hands with her flowing tears.

Above all, the venerated face of his dearly loved master rose startlingly vivid, waving to him with trembling hands, and his little travelling companion came running towards him, her dear arms outstretched in joyous greeting.

The silent army of phantoms passed and faded into space, so that amongst the falling leaves of autumn he imagined he could clearly see the many-coloured bubbles rise like tropical butterflies floating always farther away.

Last of all came Radu the shepherd, with eyes resembling two burning coals, his white teeth shining from between his smiling lips.

And there was not one of these trembling apparitions that did not look down upon him with loving glances;—only this fair being playing at his side would not turn her look his way.

Oh, those eyes that his fairy fingers at last were fixing on his canvas: deep, grey, wide open, surrounded by long black lashes that were like dark rays radiating from the unfathomed pupils, starry eyes overflowing with celestial dreams, eyes that never, ah, never would come down to look into his!

He clenched his teeth, and, casting away his brushes, he threw himself down at her feet, laying his face close against them as they rested, pale twin sisters, amongst the mosses he had gathered.

But Stella was as ever in a world of her own; and whilst the young painter was trembling with uncontrollable longing, his lips pressed upon the ground as close to her as he dared, she serenely played on her violin, making it cry out all the infinite yearning to which her ethereal nature had never yet awakened.

XXIII

And know that the sorrow of sorrows is only a law of his being.
FIONA MACLEOD.

THE tired leaves were falling always thicker; the days were shorter; night came down with the rapidity of a swooping bird; and more than once in the early morn a white frost had covered the ground like crystallized sugar strewn all over the earth.

The gypsies' camp was still pitched beside the wood. They had work to do in the villages close by, and often in the evenings the long-suffering donkeys came back heavily laden with vessels of shining copper, which the dark people mended and patched, as is the wont of their wandering race.

Their voices could be heard, either in song or strife, as they hammered away on the rounded caldrons that shone from far, the colour of molten lead.

The naked children played about in noisy groups, quarrelling like little brown monkeys, pursuing, with extended hands, every traveller that ventured too near their tents, and relating their misery with lamentable cries.

There was word of moving to some warmer clime, but as yet no order of march had been given, though the nights were cold and the large fires that were lit, and glowed in the dark like funeral pyres, were hardly sufficient protection. When the young men had finished their work for the day they would sit around in groups, playing games of cards with packs all greasy and blackened by constant use, games which often ended in noisy discord, when more than one sharpened blade would have to be knocked out of angry hands. The old women came together and sat by the leaping flames, weird witches of ancient legends, talking and chattering, relating endless yarns of endless deeds both gay and sinister, often scolding the young ones for all they had left undone, threatening them with every curse if they did not mend their ways.

The lean dogs walked about snatching at every remnant of food they could lay their hungry teeth upon, but the horses passively waited till the dark hour would sound for receiving once more their heavy burdens, which they would carry with patient resignation in spite of the scarcely healed wounds upon their tired backs.

Only Zorka never joined those rowdy groups; she sat alone in her gloomy tent like some old beggared queen, thinking about long-past glories. Her pipe was ever between her lips; the smoke curled upwards in tiny wisps, forming odd shapes that quivered about like mystic signs mounting into the damp cold air.

Each day she watched with growing anxiety the two young people, who, at the fall of night, would come slowly towards her out of the forest.

Since long she had imagined that nothing more could touch her withered heart; but the sight of these mortals, so full of beauty, purity, and light, had filled her with a new benevolence, and she longed with an unspeakable longing to help them if she could.

She was moved by conflicting feelings, asking herself if Stella's marvellous visions were worth one poor human kiss, one enchanted awakening to the wonders of love.

Oh, what use was all her long-accumulated wisdom if it failed her at a moment like this! What should she do? Should she tell the enamoured youth to go his way, not to waste his days running after something that could never be?

But it would break his heart; was he not a dreamer of dreams, and therefore a kindred soul to the solitary maiden who had never seen anything but pictures that certainly were not of this world.

Sometimes she felt an overpowering desire that a sweet miracle might come to pass, and that these two lovely innocents should both at the same instant put their lips to the full cup of Life.

Even . . . even . . . yes, death in attainment; would it be so terrible a thing! Ah! But does death ever mercifully cover with his wings two living hearts at once? Does he not always leave the one in cold misery to carry his despair alone? So many heavy problems! and she who had thought that her overburdened brain had already solved the mysteries of life! One evening she sat thus alone, pondering over all these questions to which she could find no answer.

The early dusk was descending slowly over one of autumn's last fine days, and darkness was also rising out of the cold barren earth, meeting the coming night half-way.

The sky was covered by leaden clouds, dashed by streaks of glowing red, where the sun resentfully opposed the grey shadows that strove to hide him out of sight. The air was chilly and the very old woman shivered, feeling forsaken and sad and useless.

Over the sombre expanse that lay beyond, a faint mist mounted, like fleecy wool, giving each object the appearance of floating over the earth. The tents, the gypsies that moved about, the tethered horses, the slinking dogs, all seemed to have lost their bases and to be floating in the air.

Zorka was weary, too tired to think. She was only allowing her mind to wander slowly through the past.

The fire, that young hands always built up beside her venerable grey head, leapt and sprang like restless spirits eternally striving after unattainable heights, casting fantastic lights upon her crouching form. It was a picture of old age, in all its forlorn, colourless sadness, from which all else has been taken except the weary comfort of looking back.

Zorka was remembering the distant years when she, too, had known wild love and scorching hate; when the day had been a long smile of promise, when for her also young hearts had beaten with passionate desire.

She remembered many faces that rose like ghosts out of the past, calling to her with long-forgotten voices that once she had loved. She remembered hours of triumph when the ultimate dream of happiness had arisen and wrapped her around with its burning flame.

But she had also lived through the long deadly years when nothing more was laid at her feet, when youth had carelessly trodden upon the heart that once had seemed to others a treasure impossible to obtain.

Past—past—all past; but forgotten? Dear God! ah no! But old age, weary old age from which all flee, whose breath lies like white snow upon the bended head, contains also the balm and benediction of a frosty peace that resembles the face of the night, unstarred and moonless, covering over the glaring joys and gloomy sorrows of yore!

As she was thus wandering on distant shores of her youth, a shadow crossed the space before her and she looked up. It took her a little time before she could come back to cold reality, till her brain realized that in truth she was now but Zorka the wise old witch.

Eric stood at her side; the flames flared and hissed, covering him with changing jets of light.

Between his hands he held a finished picture. Zorka gave a low cry of surprise, and rose trembling to her feet; there in the unsteady glow of the restless flames she looked upon a face the like of which human hand had never before fixed upon canvas or paper.

The eyes of the painting seemed alive, and seemed to stare with unspeakable rapture upon a sight too marvellous for poor human words to translate into mortal language. There they were with all the extraordinary beauty the hoary woman had always known : and more than all, within these eyes the dreamer of dreams had put also another expression which contained all the yearning cry of his own passionate, hopeless love.

For many a year old Zorka, the witch, had not shed a single tear—that source of emotion had dried since ages past ; but now as she gazed with quivering emotion upon the glory of this unearthly visage she felt how something rose up from her heart, warm and suffocating, clutching at her strangled throat, till one by one warm drops ran down her furrowed cheeks, leaving shining wet lines upon her leathery skin like little streams of rain on hard-baked earth.

Eric watched her, but never spoke a word ; he stood motionless, his arms hanging at his sides, tired and resigned, as one who can fight no more.

Overhead the white falcon circled and circled, uttering small weird shrieks like some one in pain ; and as it moved about in the inky sky the blue diamond round its neck shone like a moving star.

"My son," spoke Zorka at last, "thy work is great and wonderful ; and truly it could never be said of one who had fashioned so blessed a beauty that his life had been lived in vain. But I perceive that thy human longing is for ever unstilled ; and now some inner truth has broken in upon my far-seeing brain, and these are the words I have to speak to thee :

" Go to the woman that thy heart loveth too well—go, for such is the unwritten law of this earth ; go and take her in thy living arms and teach her with a kiss all the joy and all the sorrow of the world. And what the great God above desires that the end should be is not for us, who are but fashioned from His dust, to presume to foresee. Go, and I in the silence of the night shall remain here to watch and pray!"

Eric did as he was bid; laying the picture his hands had created down by the side of the reader of signs, he silently vanished into the dark.

The fire flared into a renewed burst of flame, and stretched out long arms of red glowing light as if endeavouring to call him back. Then a cold gust of wind swept over the waste and covered all around with clouds of smoke.

XXIV

*A song of deathless Love, immortal,
Sunrise-haired and starry-eyed and wondrous.*

FIONA MACLEOD.

WITHIN the tent where Stella lived each thing was sweet and pure.

Her magic charm had spread over all she touched.

Old Zorka had thus decreed that she should always have a dwelling that need be shared with none. It was as poor a place as those around, but within the folding walls was a haven of rest and peace.

On its rustic canvas sides hung all the withered wreaths that day by day she had worn. The one she had just removed from her tresses was still quite fresh, and softly swayed over the door.

Eric had found in the early morn, beneath a protecting tree, a whole bunch of scarlet strawberry leaves that the autumnal frosts had not yet touched; he had wound therefrom a lovely garland, all crimson and red, that throughout the day had crowned the loved one's brow.

A fire close by cast a friendly light through every crevice, so that the humble dwelling looked warm and homely, in spite of its barren poorness and the drear solitude upon which it stood.

Before the wide-open entry sat the mysterious maiden on an ancient wooden chest, her much-loved violin, as always, pressed tenderly beneath her cheek.

She played and played, and out of the darkness Fate was coming towards her, treading with noiseless feet. . . . Still she played on, all else forgotten or never even seen, tunes almost too sweet for human ear to bear. But to-day there was something within them resembling the sighs of a wandering soul that longs for what it cannot reach.

Something there was that perhaps the cold night air wafted to her sleeping soul—something that held a warning that the tides of life were at last gradually rising to creep close to her heart, for she suddenly laid down the faithful friend that would no more give forth the sounds she was wont to hear.

Each time she drew the bow across its melodious chords, the notes it uttered were like the cry of a lost spirit in dire distress.

So she sat gazing into the pitchy darkness with something unknown and frightening, fluttering amidst the strings of her heart. And there out of the shadows of the lonely night a human form rose and stood beside her, with arms outstretched. Then Eric was on his knees before her, and drew the slowly awakening maiden within the unbounded tenderness of his yearning arms.

The whole world seemed alive with a leaping promise of coming fulfilment.

And then, oh wonder of wonders, he laid his lips upon the heart of the girl, the girl who would not look upon his face.

And as he did so he perceived how an indescribable light of dawning comprehension spread slowly over all her features, and awoke like two luminous torches in both her eyes.

Then at last her gaze met his . . . twin flames of purest beauty, in which, quite gradually, all the hidden treasures of unconceived ecstasies rose one by one in an overwhelming flood too strong for human strength to sustain. Awful, wonderful, terrifying . . . and yet so sweet, so sweet that no halting tongue could ever describe such marvellous revelations. Almost imperceptibly she bent her angelic lips nearer his, so that the vision of his dreams was all at once looking into his upturned face, with eyes into which a God-given splendour had suddenly come in a burst of passionate understanding.

Never had the exquisite orbs been so sweet, never had the ethereal face shone with a more divine light;—and a voice that seemed to come from the far-off distances of the land of mystery pronounced these words:

"Where have I been? To what regions have I come? What is this dazzling splendour that rushes through my being like a leaping river of Life? What is this dear face I see gazing into mine, what is this bounding joy that wants to burst the confines of my overstrained heart? Oh what—oh what does it mean?"

Drawing herself up she stood, both hands pressed on her heaving breast, as if her great pain were piercing her through and through.

"What is it? . . . what is it? . . . What can it be? I do not understand!"

Eric rose also, and stood trembling before this unheard-of miracle that had come to pass.

A great fear came to him and swept with a cold wind over his immensity of joy. Would she suddenly close her mind again to his flaming love, now that he had at last aroused her sleeping soul?

"Oh, my love, my love!" he cried. "It is I, it is I, who have come over the distant seas, who have travelled through sun and shade, through storm and calm, who have passed through the Shadow of Death to reach the heaven of thy face; look at me with thy awakening eyes, and tell me that life is sweet."

"Life!" said the girl, her two hands still tightly clutching at her pulsing heart.

"Life, what is Life?"

"Life," cried Eric, "is contained in this one hour of perfect attainment. Life is the great promise of love fulfilled. Life is the sacred moment when my arms may clasp thee to my thirsting soul!

"Come, my beloved, for I have waited so cruelly long, so tirelessly have I searched and yearned!"

Stella, moved by some unknown, mysterious force, timidly drew near to this stranger man, whose face was as fair as the angels with whom in her visions she had always dwelt.

But what was this waking joy — this tumultuous tide of intensest bliss? Something too strong, too strong, something that no living mortal could bear. . . . And yet now she lay within his passionate arms, her head hidden against his throbbing straining heart.

In an agony of delight no words can describe, his lips, his warm living lips, were drinking her very soul away—drawing by slow degrees her sweet hardly-dawning life to mix with his boundless need.

He knew that this was the ultimate limit of his soul's desire, a moment of such incommensurable joy, that body and soul flowed together into a sunrise of dazzling triumph. All that had been, was as if it had never existed. Past, present, and future were caught up and welded together into a blaze of unearthly rapture.

He felt that he was being carried by the eternal wings of creation into the very heart of the throbbing world; he was one with Nature, he was one with God, one with his whole being's most sacred longing. And thus, closely locked in each other's arms, these two mortals of perfect beauty lived an hour that lies as a pulsing memory, deeply hidden within the dark lap of the ever-wakeful Mother Earth, and from which it rose like a song of undying, eternal perfection to the vastness of the sky above : a song that now floats in never-ending echoes on every passing cloud, on every ray of the sun. It was an hour when Nature stood still to listen to the accomplishment of one of her dearest dreams—when all life seemed concentrated within the happiness of those two frail human beings. . . .

A cold streak of dawn was slowly advancing with pale furtiveness out of the cover of night, when Eric bent once again to press his lips upon the perfect mouth ; as he did so Stella looked up into his face with those eyes that had for so long been a living part of his most hidden self.

Oh ! was ever any earthly thing so marvellous, so wonderful, as those two grey stars of light ! and a sweet whisper rose stealing into every drop of his blood :

"I love thee, I love thee, as never have I loved a single one of my heavenly dreams ; I have learnt in this hour the most limitless boundaries of human bliss. Lay now thy dear lips upon these eyes thou hast found at last, so that no other sight than thy fond face may ever trouble my inner vision.

"Oh, see the day dawns ; give me once more all thy bounding soul in the blessing of thy kiss."

Eric lifted the beloved woman and pressed her in a frenzy of joy to his heart ; then very gently laid his mouth upon her eyes, closing the delicate lids, shutting away within her starry orbs the visage she loved more than all else.

Long did he remain thus holding her sweet face beneath his tender caress, whilst a heavenly smile parted her gentle lips.

And it seemed to Eric that at that moment his life and hers were flowing quietly together in one great tide towards the shores of Eternity. . . .

But when old Zorka came at the break of day to see how her dear ones fared, she stood strangling a cry that rose in the air ; then, throwing herself upon the ground, she hid her grey head in the dust.

There sat Eric with wandering gaze, his eyes wide open, full of frantic misery, looking down upon a corpse he held pressed closely to his beating heart. And through the gold of his shining locks, soft silver threads were scattered like finely spun moonbeams entwined with the rays of the sun.

Zorka lifted her haggard face and stared in awe at the ghost-like pallor of the girl. A wonderful light rested on her waxen features as she lay full of peace and rest, white and motionless in the arms of her lover.

Her eyes were closed as one who has shut her tired lids over a joy too great for words, the vastness of which had burst asunder her human heart.

XXV

> And thy first night of death
> Belongs to our first sorrow. . . .
> What knowledge now is thine?
> A deeper one than ours.
>
> BARD OF THE DÂMBOVITZA.

ALL day the dark men of the tribe had been building a coffin into which the beautiful maiden was to be laid to rest.

One and all were bowed with sorrow; this death was to them a horrible unreality their simple minds could not grasp. Why was this creature of light cut down in her sweetest prime?

What would their lives now be without the glamour and mystery with which she had filled their wandering day?

The morning was bleak, and the rain fell in occasional showers that the wind swept, with moaning sighs, over the naked waste. The canvas of the tents flapped and creaked, straining against the poles and cords that held them in place.

A heavy gloom brooded over the wretched camp, so that even the squabbling children spoke with bated breath.

Within Stella's silent tent sat Eric of the golden locks, staring without tears upon the face of the dead. The eyes of his dream looked upon him no more; he had shut them for ever with the passion of his kiss. Beneath his living lips she had breathed her last, dying like a fading flower, scorched by the flame of his love!

He had not known when she had passed away—only the growing chill he had felt beneath his cheek had pierced his soul with a sudden fear, and when he had called on her beloved name no answer had come in response. But we shall draw a veil over that hour of morn when he realized what was to be his fate. There are times of darkness and bottomless grief wherein the eye of a stranger must never descend. This was the end—the end! Hope was dead, life was a waste, and all had been but a passionate dream that ended with a kiss !

The wind swept over the humble tent, but upon her lowly couch Stella still smiled the wise smile that removes the dead so far beyond the reach of those who weep.

Not far off sat Zorka, the witch, her head bent down upon her trembling knees, whilst the storm played amongst the frosted wisps of her hair. From all sides weird chants rose into the wintry air where the old women, sitting round their blazing fire, were singing dirges for the dead.

And now came the moment when the black-eyed, black-haired sons of the wild came to carry Stella to her last narrow bed.

They had fashioned her a coffin with sides of shining copper the colour of the autumn that had now passed away. Eric had to stand by and see how they lifted the body he loved, and laid it, all rigid and small, within the three sides of the metal box that received in unmoved silence this, his faded dream.

The gypsies had sullenly refused to let him carry her himself; they jealously desired to have at least her inert body within their arms, they who had never dared touch a single hair of her head.

They did not know that she had died beneath the kiss of his lips, but they somehow guessed that at the end he had awakened her sleeping soul; and although they had dearly loved his beautiful face, Eric had always been an alien in their midst, all shining and fair, a being of light amongst their sombre race.

Now she was dead—Stella was dead—the Luck of their

tribe lay white and cold in her last resting-place. Now she was theirs, and this son of another clime must relinquish his right, and leave her pure perfection between their dusky hands.

So while they were carrying her from out her tent Eric wandered with dragging feet into the forest where he had so often sat, painting her lovely face.

Now all the gold had fallen to the ground, the trees stood gaunt and bare. Over his cruelly bowed head the branches stretched naked and grey; from every twig large dropping tears fell splashing on the carpet of faded leaves.

Nowhere could he find the smallest plant or flower out of which to wind her a final wreath the same as those she had always worn. In vain he searched each sheltered corner; wherever he peered, all was dark and dead, killed by the frost of the night.

When he came back to where she lay, pale and still, all that he had to bring to the woman he loved was a crown of thorns. These he pressed on her snowy brow where they rested, sharp and hard, amongst her silky tresses, so that verily she resembled a martyred queen upon the bier of a beggar.

In a circle around her coffin the gypsies had lighted blazing fires, and now that their work was done they left the stranger standing in lonely communion with that silent shape that never again would look upon the light of day.

As he knelt beside her lowly bed, his face hidden on the heart that beat no more, a sound of wings came wafted upon the wind, and there, fluttering above the lifeless maiden, was his trusted companion the milk-white hawk, holding in its sharpened beak the chain with the moon-coloured diamond.

As Eric looked up with hopeless eyes, he saw how the beautiful creature swooped down quite close, covering the lovely vision with its large soft wings; and when it rose again, like foam against the darkening sky, Gundian espied upon the heart of the maiden the magic diamond, shining as if all her love were a last time bursting from her breast in mystic rays of enchantment.

Night came down and still Eric knelt beside his shattered happiness. All about him the fires burned and crackled, and the dismal chants of the gypsies rose like curses to the heavens.

The wondrous face of the sleeper lived again in the glowing shine, but Eric did not see this illusive light of life; when he looked up the fires had burnt out; the gypsies had gone to rest.

The night had laid its darkness over the frowning solitude; no star shone in the sky; the only spot of brightness was the twinkling diamond that glowed there on Stella's bosom, where Eric had awakened her soul with his first burning kiss of love!

XXVI

The grey wind weeps, the grey wind weeps, the grey wind weeps.
Dust on her breast, dust on her eyes,
The grey wind weeps.
FIONA MACLEOD.

NEXT day her grave was dug, there, upon that endless plain of silence. Eric had strewn the gaping hole with a lining of withered leaves, gathered from the weeping forest.

Before they hid her marvellous face out of sight he had passionately covered its mask of beauty with desperate burning kisses. Zorka had stood close by, guarding him from hostile glances, so that this heartbroken lover might be for a last time alone with what had been the dream of his life.

Then from his shoulders he took the torn black cloak he had worn during all his wanderings and draped it round those rigid limbs that froze his blood with their icy coldness.

"Mother, dear old mother," he cried, "I want to keep her warm; the night before last she glowed in the arms of my passion, and now I must leave her to the chill mercy of the frozen ground. How can I bear such torture?"

Zorka laid her withered hand upon his shoulder.

"Son, my son, I feel that no ice can harm her more—she looked upon the flames of Love, and died whilst they were folded round her; she closed her eyes upon the vision of thy burning worship, and that wonderful sweetness was the last thing she saw; now she is for ever happy."

So Eric wound her from head to foot in the dark folds of

his mantle ; he hid away her white hands and her tiny feet. Then he pressed the wreath of thorns over the dusky drapery, placing the gleaming gem in the centre of her forehead. He fetched her dear violin and laid it so that her toes just touched its polished wood.

Over the shabby black tissue of the weather-beaten vestment he spread the faded wreaths that once had rested upon her rippling hair. And after one long look of farewell he allowed the heavy lid to be shut down on his hard-won happiness.

The damp earth was thrown with a hollow thud over the lid of the coffin, the ground was beaten down smooth and flat on every side, so that no wandering stranger should ever disturb her deep dark grave beneath its covering of sombre soil.

The gypsies folded their tents with hasty rapidity, longing to steal away from a place where silence brooded amongst the whispering winds.

Old Zorka came and stood upon the spot where her darling had been hidden for ever away, and there she murmured all the prayers she could call back to her flagging memory, whilst her streaming tears mixed with the mould that lay over that past dream of beauty.

But no persuasion nor entreaty could make Eric move from that dark mound in the barren lonely wild ; he meant to remain there that first night when she had been confided to the indifferent shadows that closed in around her.

He promised Zorka he would follow next day, but this night he must lie on Stella's cold grave, to protect it from the biting frost.

When all had gone and he was alone on that dreary vastness, he drew from its sheath his treasured sword and planted it like a cross, there where her eyes must be hidden away, never more to look upon the rising sun.

Dreary blasts of wind blew over the gloomy desert ; darkness came down and Eric stretched himself upon the frozen ground, his lips pressed upon the spot where, far beneath the heavy covering of soil, her beautiful mouth must have been.

There he lay, forsaken, the only breathing being in that cruel night of sorrow. But not far off, amongst the dim shadows of the forest, the snowy falcon was faithfully watching, though the glinting light no longer shone on his breast, watching till day should mercifully break.

Through the heavy hours Eric never moved; he was fighting alone a dreary battle against life and his God. Nor did he know, as his face lay hidden in his clenched hands, that the magic hilt of the sword was glowing like a shining promise far over the sleeping world. There it stood, a cross of flame, burning with sacred light, watching over this desperate mortal who longed to cast his life away.

The wind howled with voices of terror and storm; the dust was whirled in clouds from the frozen waste, sweeping over the cross-shaped light and over the weeping man, trying to blot them out of sight.

But deep down in eternal night, under the protecting arms of her lover, rested Stella in stony quiet, bedded in the lap of old Mother Earth.

Beneath her closed lids her starry eyes were for ever guarding the last dear vision her waking brain had looked upon.

XXVII

And in her two white hands like swans on a frozen lake,
Hath she not my heart, that I have hidden there for dear love's sake.
                                                    FIONA MACLFOD

MORNING dawned, and Eric rose from the ground, half-frozen from his long night's vigil, his eyes hollow, staring with a desperate look.

The wan daylight was gradually spreading over the wilderness, on which he stood like a wounded soldier whom his comrades had forsaken, imagining he was dead. No, he was not dead, poor youth, he was alive, crying, with broken heart and thirsting soul, for what could be no more. He had lived his dream and shattered it all in one. Zorka had been right, some flowers must not be plucked; and now his hands were empty—empty. He himself had made the sweet petals fall, and no earthly power could give them back their bloom.

Down there under the dark cold sod she lay, his dream of dreams, crushed by his passion and love. He had held his soul's desire pressed against his wildly beating heart, and she had left him in their hour of rapture; had died beneath the fire of his kiss.

Once more he threw himself down upon the merciless earth that covered her sacred beauty. He pressed his mouth upon the dust of the ground, tracing the sign of the Cross with his lips, there where he guessed that her snowy brow, her silent heart, and closed eyes lay hidden for ever out of sight.

Then kneeling before the cross-shaped sword, Eric prayed

in words of glowing entreaty to the great Father above, that her sleep should be sweet and the earth soft to that body he loved, that the weight of the dark mould that wrapped her round should not be heavy to her delicate limbs.

He cried to that silent brooding sky to be merciful towards that creature of light and soon to call her from the damp dark grave to a sunrise of glory and joy.

"God! my God! it cannot be that Thou lettest her slumber for ever in that cold solitude and I not knowing if her sleep be sweet. She who was like a ray from the sun—she who carried within her orbs the whole glory of the summer skies, the entire mystery of the starry nights. She whose music was the most exquisite rendering of the beauty of life; she whose perfection was the gladness of each awakening day, whose soul and body were like the spotless snow of mountain heights where no human foot has ever passed. O God! O God! how can I leave her grave?" And again he lay there, stretched upon the relentless soil, groaning and shedding tears of blood, whilst the brooding silence of the naked wild lay over all, hostile and unheeding, with Nature's stony indifference to the sorrow and anguish of the human race.

Then at last he tore himself away, feeling how useless were his grief and misery before those eternal laws of creation which for ever are, and for ever shall be.

Now he was fleeing that silent wilderness, bending his head against the driving wind and rain, against the storm of dust and sand that the wild gusts were throwing in his face.

Several times he turned in hopeless yearning towards that lonesome spot where his precious sword stood a lonely guardian of his lost happiness; then, covering his face in an agony too deep for tears, on he rushed as one who tries to escape from a sight he cannot bear.

His faithful friend the hawk flew beside him, occasionally

caressing his tear-stained face with the velvet touch of its wings.

For several hours he had thus fought his desperate way, when, on raising his head, he saw a small cloud coming towards him out of the distance, growing in size the nearer it came.

He stood still, vaguely wondering what it might be, when out of the midst of the moving dust a young boy emerged, driven along by the storm that strove to carry him off his feet.

The first thing Eric discerned was a high fur cap, a shaggy coat of skins, into the wide sleeves of which the youth's hands had been deeply thrust, whilst a thick staff was pressed in the hollow of his arm. Behind this advancing figure came the pattering feet of innumerable sheep, raising beneath their steps the thick cloud Eric had first of all descried.

Suddenly, with a glad cry, both youths ran towards each other with joyful recognition, for this was none other than Radu, the shepherd, who was leading his flocks home from the mountains, driven thence by the coming winter.

For a moment both remained speechless, hands clasped, staring into each other's face that were wet and shining from the drizzling rain which had not yet been able to turn into mud the thick coating of dust that lay like powder on the roads. The one who spoke first was Radu, and it was anxiously to ask:

" Where hast thou left thy cloak? Thou art quite wet; and thy sword, thy beautiful sword, where hast thou left thy sword?"

Eric did not answer; he simply lifted both his hands, showing that they were empty; then he let them fall again at his sides with the hopeless gesture of one who has given everything up for ever more. Then only did Radu come quite near and peer with frightened eyes more closely into his face.

" What is it?" he cried. " What is it? What hast thou seen?"

"Heaven and Hell," answered Eric. "I have been in both!"

"And thy dream—didst thou find thy dream?" whispered the peasant.

"I found it and I lost it," was the answer he got. "It was mine for a short hour of bliss—mine; but again God beat me down with my face to the earth.

"I have been a dreamer of dreams, and it is not to be given to me to keep what I clasp. God allowed me visions to lead me ever on; they brought me to this land of promise.

"It was summer then; now thou seest what colour is over the earth. But I touched my dream; I held it within my human arms; but as sayeth the poet: 'How can the body touch the flower which only the spirit may touch,' so I killed my flower, killed it with my kiss."

"Can one kill with a kiss?" cried Radu, awe in his voice.

"One can kill with more things than with a sword. I found the face of my vision, I followed it step by step. I hunted it down with sighs and tears till at last it was mine. I held it one short moment in my arms, a moment within which I lived the ultimate triumph of my desire. Then it was gone. I myself destroyed it, consumed it, with the thirst of my soul!"

"But was she happy?" queried Radu, with tears in his eyes.

"Was she happy! Good God! was she happy!" cried Eric, clenching his fists towards the skies. "Yes, I believe she was happy! If I did not believe that I could not live. She said to me to kiss her eyes so that for ever she could keep the picture of what she had loved best in this world! At that moment she died! My warm touch of love was death! Canst grasp that frightful truth? . . . was death! My lips, my lover's lips closed her eyes for ever! . . . for ever . . . over the vision of my face!

"Before they laid her in the ground I wrapped her in my cloak; that is why it is gone. I would not leave her thus thinly clad within the cold shadow of her grave; and upon the spot where she lies I planted my sword. There, where the eyes I followed so far are for ever closed, I left my sword."

"Oh," sobbed Radu, "and now I shall never see that face!"

"Yes, thou shalt," answered his friend. "Come with me and thou shalt see the fairest being God ever made!"

"Where?" asked the astonished peasant, "where?"

"Follow me and thou shalt know!"

"But my sheep,—they are tired; and see how tame are my dogs, exhausted by the length of the way."

"It is not far from here—there thou canst rest; thou art not in a hurry, and I would thou shouldst know the eyes of my dream."

Again Eric hid his face in his clasped hands, whilst a harsh dry sob rose to his throat.

"Come, come! I, too, thirst for the sight of her face."

Towards the evening the two lads arrived at the gypsies' camp.

Along the dreary roadside several tall wooden crosses had been erected, tall and gaunt, with curious shapes, decorated with archaic saints in crudest colours.

These weird crosses stood in a line like silent spectres, some bending sideways, as if tired of their vigil.

It was here that old Zorka had told Eric he would find their halting-place. The fires had already been lit, the dark men and women sat about in groups. The tents stood out, dismal shadows, against the Western Bar.

Eric holding Radu by the hand led him to where Zorka was cooking her evening meal in a blackened pot.

Radu's flock had followed pitter-patter in their wake, hardly discernible in the dusk, their way-stained wool the colour of the ground they trod.

When she saw her favourite the old seer ran forward and clasped him to her breast, anxiously scanning his haggard face, but saying never a word for fear of awakening his surging grief.

"Mother Zorka," he said, "here is a friend who has come to look upon her face!"

Zorka went to her tent, brought out the wonderful picture, and put it into the peasant's hands. He stared at it in enraptured silence. Then very slowly he laid it on the ground and knelt before it, making the sign of the cross over his brow, the tears flowing down his cheeks.

Zorka brought the boys food in a dish, urging her dear one to eat, but Eric shook his head.

"Mother Zorka, willst thou tend him and give him a bed? for he was good to me when I was in sore distress."

Then taking the picture he went off alone in the darkness of the night. The wind howled, and the rain came down in heavier showers, beating upon the miserable tents.

Zorka sat with the young shepherd in the shelter of her dwelling, looking out upon the darkness into which the lonely mourner had disappeared.

"Was she an angel?" asked Radu, who had finished his meal, and whose face was still wet with tears.

"I think she was," said Zorka, nodding her head.

"Tell me," he continued, "why did she die?"

"Why did she die?" repeated the tired old woman. "Because it is given to some never to wake from their dream of bliss, and those it is said are loved of the gods."

"Why was he left alone? Do the gods not love him?"

Zorka sighed: "Because some must learn to the bitter end to overcome all they reach; must learn to leave behind them both joy and pain ; to rise above all their desires, and hopes, and fears, till their souls are as pure and bright as an archangel's sword ; and those are the chosen of God."

" But was she happy ? " queried Radu, for the second time.

" Yes," answered Zorka, with a solemn voice. " Yes, she was happy. She died of joy."

XXVIII

*A star has ceased to shine in my lonely skies,
Sometimes I dream I see it shining in my heart.*
FIONA MACLEOD.

ZORKA could not bear to part from Eric of the golden locks, and begged him to remain at her side.

He, too, for a while felt that he dared not leave the old woman who had led him to his love; so all that winter he wandered about with the travelling clan, from clime to clime, leaving far behind him the country of his dream. Wherever he went the falcon followed, flying as near his head as it could.

Radu had parted from Eric with tears in his eyes; both boys felt as they joined hands for the last time that nothing could wipe out the deep affection they had conceived for each other.

Radu had gone off on an endless road, playing a melancholy tune on his wooden flute, his flock following him, his cowed dogs at his heels, his feet splashing about in the mud, the patient sheep leaving thousands of small footprints wherever they passed.

But Eric played no more, neither did he sing; and over the gold of his locks the silver began to spread more and more, like foam on the sea.

Wherever he stopped he bought canvas and paint, but each of his pictures showed always but the one and only face.

He painted the features of his dream in every form his heart could remember.

He represented her as first he had seen her, crowned with a wreath of bells, her old violin pressed under her cheek, her eyes full of the visions she alone could see. He painted her seated in the dust of the road with a circle of corn-ears round her delicate brow. He conjured up her beauty against the setting sun, whilst the coronet she wore was of autumn leaves all glowing as the blazing sky.

One of his sketches showed her shimmering and pale, lit by the rays of the moon, and this time it was a halo he had painted round the pureness of her heavenly face.

And once his restless fingers had created the picture of her marble features as she lay motionless on her bier, her face still and white under the brooding clouds, with the crown of thorns on her head, her wonderful eyes closed beneath the heavy lids, a smile of peace and happiness hovering like a blessing over her lips.

But one picture alone no human eye but his was ever allowed to see; on that one he had awakened, for a second and last time, the look her eyes had borne when he had closed them with his lips.

This sketch he kept jealously hidden beneath all the others, and it was never shown—not even Zorka had the right to cast a glance upon that expression which was too holy for mortal to look upon.

One of his pictures he had given to Zorka in sign of gratitude. It represented the lost Luck of the wandering tribe. She stood on a lonely plain, her hands joined behind her back, her eyes looking straight before her, her head slightly raised as if listening for the coming of a being she could not see.

A marvellous picture of unearthly beauty before which the old fortune-teller daily said her curious prayers, prayers to a God who had no form, but who lived in every breath of the wind, and who filled her weary old soul with the hope of coming peace.

They wandered slowly from land to land, amidst scenes of beauty, and often also through countries bleak and joyless ; but the heart of the painter was always yearning for a far-off desolate plain where he had planted his shining sword over the face of his love.

When at night he closed his lids over his eyes heavy with unshed tears, that wilderness always rose before him, cold and lonely, filling him with a haunting dread that the sword might be slowly descending to pierce her innocent heart. That vision would suddenly awake him out of his sleep, and horror would stand at the foot of his wretched bed, till he could bear it no more and would rush wildly out into the night.

Zorka knew all his suffering, and bowed her head always lower to the ground.

When spring was covering the earth with a new smile of youth, Zorka felt that the moment she dreaded had come, and that the loved wanderer would soon leave her to go his way.

She had heard him speak of a wonderful picture he was one day to finish in the palace of a mighty king. With her seer's certainty she knew that the time was close at hand— had he not found the face of love,—and slowly the desire must strengthen within him to terminate the work he had begun.

She accepted the coming of this final suffering as one who knows that her days are surely numbered.

One morning Eric Gundian, the last joy of her eyes, stood tall and slim before her dimmed sight.

"Mother Zorka, I feel I must go. I thank thee for all thy bounteous kindness, and I want thy blessing as once the dear master gave me his ! "

He knelt down as a little child might have done, and laid the frosted gold of his locks amongst the folds of her earth-coloured rags. She placed her trembling hands upon his head and raised her quavering voice :

"Go in peace, my loved one, take up thy burden and finish thy great work ; it is thy duty to return to the kingly master who loved thee so well, and when thy pain seems too heavy to bear, remember these words of old Zorka the witch.

"Those who die of happiness are blessed, but thrice blessed is the man who carries without complaint the burden of his broken heart. Thou hast known the sublimest fulfilment of joy. Be for ever grateful for that hour of bliss, and remember that she died at the moment of attainment, which is given to so few ; therefore do not mourn as if her lot had been cruel. There are others who fall before winning the race ; thou hast known what it is to reach thy goal ; so, thou must not weep. Go, and carry joy with thee wherever thou treadest, because thou art a Chosen of God. It is I, the old seer, who thus does speak."

She bent low over him and pressed her quivering lips to the silver threads in his hair ; then he rose, and stood with his head thrown back, his arms reaching up towards the vault of blue, as one who longs to be received within the far-off clouds.

"But, Mother Zorka, I can sing no more ; God has drowned my voice in a sea of tears ! "

"My son, thou hast thy wonderful art. Go and live amongst those who believe in thee. Thou hast a great work to complete, and the face of thy love shall shine for ever upon the generations to come. This thou canst still do for her memory's sake, and that power is given to few.

"There was a time when I believed I ought to guard our beautiful Stella from all touch of mortal love ; but now I know that thus it is best. Each human being must fulfil his destiny, and Stella's destiny was to be the realization of thy dream.

"The days of each man's life are counted, and not any of

our poor knowledge can add an hour to the length of time Fate has decreed we should live.

"Thou didst not kill her with thy kiss; she lived as a flower from some unknown land, yielding her sweet perfume to but one single being; then God took her for His own, and thus her life was to end. Cry not out against what had to be. Go thy way, and one day perhaps thou wilt know the meaning which now our mortal mind cannot fathom. My blessing is with thee. Go in peace."

And that day Eric Gundian left the dark wandering people and old Zorka the witch.

When he had reached the crest of a hill he turned round and waved to the trembling old woman who had been so faithful a friend.

Over his head his inseparable companion fluttered like a snow-white sail caught by the wind.

Zorka stood leaning on her crooked staff, her hand raised to protect her eyes, that were blinded with tears, against the glare of the rising sun.

She stood watching the departing youth she had so dearly loved, and it seemed to her that he walked away from her straight into the glittering sky.

XXIX

Spring in all its beauty was covering the world with blossoms pink and white. Within the tender sprouting grass pale anemones were raising their delicate faces to peep at the radiant sun. Humble sweet-smelling violets covered the lawns with a carpet of richest hue. Everywhere the birds were singing hymns of praise to the sweet resurrection of life and joy. The larks were for ever mounting into the sky in eternal adoration of the shining sun.

A haze of green was beginning to spread over the awakening woods, and innumerable flowers were pushing out their tiny heads from beneath the thick carpet of fallen leaves. Over all lay a sweet hush of promise, timid yet spreading far and wide.

King Wanda sat upon his marble terrace basking in the first warmth of the season. Close beside him was Oona in a new dress of gold, a marvellous book upon her knees containing pictures in glowing colours, relating of fairies, both good and bad. She piped away with sweet clear voice, explaining all the wonders she saw; but King Wanda sat with a frown on his brow; nothing seemed to bring a smile to his lips; he had become morose and silent, and vainly his courtiers had tried to replace the favourite who had so suddenly left him long ago.

King Wanda could find no joy since that day when Eric Gundian, the mad painter, had gone from his palace in search of his dream. He had given up all hope of seeing him again, although many a night he lay tossing upon his kingly couch, harking if he could not discern some sound of the step that once he had loved.

Other painters had proposed to finish the frieze in the beautiful hall, but sternly the King had repressed their zeal. He himself kept the keys of that now silent chamber, and none save himself had entry through those massive doors. He raised his head as some one came towards him over the sunlit terrace. It was a page, and this was the news he brought. Outside the palace doors a stranger was standing in the garb of a beggar, demanding admittance, saying he had come to do King Wanda's bidding, and entreating to be allowed to speak to the master himself.

"He is all travel-stained," said the page, "and upon his back he carries a load wrapped in a cloth. His feet are bare, his head uncovered, his clothes all torn and soiled; within his hands he bears a staff wrought with unknown designs. The hair on his head is long and covered with dust, and his eyes are horribly sad; most strange of all, upon the beggar's shoulder a curious bird is quietly seated. In truth the man seems to have come from the end of the earth."

"I will have word with him," said the King, "as it is his desire to talk with me. Am I not here for all those who call at my door? None, it shall be said, go unconsoled or are sent away without receiving their heart's desire."

Now the tattered traveller was standing upon the terrace before the presence of the King. His load had been laid upon the marble floor. The white bird sat motionless upon his shoulder, like a ghost in a dream. The rays of the sun shone upon his bent head, and as they lit on the long locks of the stranger's hair, making them sparkle and flash in the light, King Wanda gave a sudden cry, clutching at his heart. Then he sprang forward, and all the courtiers were witness of an astounding sight: a beggar lying against the heart of their King, who was sobbing as if his heart would break!

And then Eric was on his knees, his head hidden in the hands of the good old King he had left to wander so far away. He was telling the crowned man that he had come back to finish the picture he had once begun, because now he knew what was the face of the woman who sat on the golden throne.

"Give me leave, O most royal master, to complete the work of my hands; but let me tell thee that Eric Gundian, thy singing-bird, died one early morn under an alien sky at the break of day—it is only his spirit that has come to thee, because the Dreamer of Dreams has a last great wish to paint the face of love upon thy gilded walls!"

So the King himself led the weary wanderer into his gorgeous hall, unlocking the heavy door with the key that hung from his waist.

Like a soft white cloud the falcon glided into the room before them, settling upon the tall stone fire-place, whence it watched the strangely assorted couple.

When alone together, for the first time Eric of the golden locks raised his haggard face and looked straight into the eyes of the King.

The old man felt as though a dagger were piercing his heart when he met that hopeless gaze. Certainly those were the features of the boy he had loved, but oh, what was it he had gone through to be so cruelly changed? His cheeks were hollow, the sunken orbs stared with a far-away look too sad for the language of men, and his golden hair was covered with a fine web of silver that lay like an early frost over a ripe field of corn.

Long did King Wanda stand mute, not finding a word; he felt that he stood in presence of a grief so deep that he dared not come too near. It was Eric who spoke:

"May I remain within thy palace, O King, to complete the work that once I began? I feel that now I can verily put the finishing touches to a picture that in ages past was the pride of my painter's art.

"And above all, I crave thy pardon for having left thee on that summer's morn so long ago. It must have seemed as if I were void of both gratitude and love, but it was not thus.

"I have wandered far, and have returned from the regions of dreams to fulfil the task that thou didst once demand of me, so that thy belief in Eric Gundian should not have been in vain! I see by thy look, O most royal master, that still thou dost trust in me."

"May the completing of thy work bring peace to thy heart!" was the King's reply; and once more he drew the dusty wayfarer within his fatherly arms. Within a few days Eric was again established in his old place, working with all his soul.

King Wanda had given orders that he should be left entirely undisturbed; and there he painted from early morn as long as the daylight lasted. Even King Wanda dared not trouble his peace—he had a feeling that this work was being done with a love that no stranger's eye should watch.

Indeed, it was with his very life's blood that the painter was now completing his masterpiece; he felt that each day he was giving some of his strength—that little by little his force was going with each fresh stroke of his brush.

At times his face was corpse-like, as one no more of this earth.

Once little Oona had peeped through an opening in the

window-curtain, and had then run quickly back, with a feeling that she had seen a ghost.

But the face that Eric was creating upon King Wanda's wall was of a beauty no words can describe.

The woman on the throne, with the golden dress that flowed down like a river seen at sunset, was leaning slightly forward, her eyes looking away over the heads of the crowd that was calling upon her name in praise.

She seemed to see no one; but other visions more beautiful than earthly eyes could conceive filled her gaze. The two palms of her hands were pressed down at her side in a strained attitude, as one who is half afraid, or perhaps awakening to some astounding knowledge.

But her eyes was the spot within which Eric Gundian had concentrated all his inimitable art : they were the most marvellous wells of light and shade that had ever been painted by mortal hand.

They were a mighty realization of his eternal dream—that dream that had led him through distant countries and deadly dangers to the very fount of love. Eric now lived only sustained by his feverish desire to leave those eyes, he had so loved, for ever upon that frieze that would be a living incorporation of his one great aim.

But behind those shut doors he was wasting away ; he was but a spirit whose body was an overcome burden, living by the soul alone, only a breath of that human life he had spent in the eternal effort to reach his glorious dream. Near by sat the snow-white hawk, who would never leave his side except for short moments when Eric opened the window, upon the beauties of spring, letting the bird out to search for its daily food.

Eric himself seemed to dread the light of the sun ; neither would he eat of the royal dishes that were brought him ; he sipped from time to time a little water, otherwise he lived sustained by the love of his work.

Eric Gundian—Eric of the golden locks—was now but a wavering breath, kept alive by the desire to finish his wonderful picture.

One morning, when all had been stiller than usual behind those silent walls, King Wanda, with anxious face, opened the heavy door—and there, upon the ground, stretched all his length before his finished masterpiece, lay Eric Gundian, the dreamer of dreams, his wet brush still clasped in his hand.

Near him, as always, sat the strange white bird watchfully motionless, but this time there were actually tears in its piercing eyes.

The lids of the dreamer were closed for ever, as one, dead-tired, who mercifully has found rest at last. . . .

But on the golden throne of the picture sat a woman more beautiful than any brain can conceive,—within the expression of her eyes lay a world of joy and sorrow, that had blended into a look of unearthly glory impossible to describe.

King Wanda stood staring, unable to move, overcome with a sorrow too deep for words; yet he had the feeling that whoso had been able to accomplish such a miracle could only die at the moment of attainment, because such a marvel must verily be paid for by the life of the one who thus was allowed to create it.

All the courtiers now came trooping together and stood in awe behind their King, staring and whispering, hushed by the dark mystery they could not understand.

Then a murmur went from lip to lip.

"Oh, why has the marvellous woman a crown of thorns upon her head? Why, oh why did he paint the face of Love crowned with a wreath of thorns?"

King Wanda bowed his weary head: then he knelt on the

floor and kissed the brow of the favourite he had loved so well—and, looking into that pale and silent face, he thought he understood what the Dreamer had meant when, with the last touch of his brush, he had crowned Love's immaculate visage with a wreath of thorns.

XXX

And Beauty, Peace, and Sorrow are dreams within dreams
                              Fiona Macleod.

In a distant land Spring was also spreading over hill and dale.

But on a bare plain, where nothing grew, a miracle had come to pass: a peasant, returning home one starry night, had espied, from the road upon which he was slowly sauntering, a strange light in the form of a cross, gleaming far over the barren waste.

Full of astonishment he had run to the spot, and there he had discerned a magic crystal, all charged with radiance, in the shape before which every Christian bends the knee. And the most curious of all, this burning cross was the hilt of a glistening sword which must have dropped from heaven, to remain thus firmly planted in the ground.

Awed and filled with wonder the youth had spread the astounding news from village to village, and all the simple folk had run together, falling down in worship before this miraculous sign, which God had put in so desert a place, as a blessing on the land.

From far and wide, rich and poor, old and young, men, women, and children came in pilgrimage to that holy site.

None ever knew, except one humble little peasant, from whence the cross had come.

But Radu, the shepherd, held his peace, thanking the Kind Mother of Christ for having thus ordained that so many pious believers should go and pray on the grave where the dreamer of dreams had buried his love.

One morning when the warm rays of the sun were lying like a blessing over the deserted waste, a white bird might have been seen descending out of the blue.

It hovered for a time over the gleaming sword, circling very slowly, so that its outspread wings resembled a snowy cloud floating in the air.

Then down it swooped out of the heavens, there, where Stella lay beneath the dark heavy mould. Within its beak this unknown bird was holding a simple seed, which it dropped on the very spot where the dead girl's heart rested under the sod—a seed it had carried from a distant land of the north from the tenderly tended grave in a great king's garden. Hardly had the seed touched the barren earth than it sprang up and spread all over the tomb a thick network of rambling thorns covered with countless roses—as crimson as the broken heart of a lover.

And these roses bloomed, even in the winter months, upon the icy covering of snow, red as the reddest blood, till all the simple folk declared that indeed the place was Holy Ground.

And thus it was that God blessed the Love of him who once had been called Eric Gundian, the Dreamer of Dreams.

THE END

Printed in Great Britain by R. & R. CLARK, LIMITED, *Edinburgh*

Lightning Source UK Ltd.
Milton Keynes UK
UKHW051249070620
364497UK00008B/52